NO SECRETS

No
Secrets

A Young Lady's Search for Answers

THE THIRD IN THE THORNTON TRILOGY

MARY CHRISTIAN PAYNE

Published by TCK Publishing
www.TCKPublishing.com

Sign up for the newsletter to get news, updates and new release info from Mary Christian Payne:
http://bit.ly/MaryChristianPayne

To Lesley for Immeasurable Help and Instructions about Knickers

1

Chloe Thornton, richly clad in a stunning coat and dress ensemble, walked slowly down the winding staircase from the second level at Highcroft Hall. She fastened her coat as she moved. The top button was stubborn, and she paused on the landing to give it her undivided attention. The filtered light from the stained glass window shined down into a beam of illumination and gave a vivid touch to the little golden purse she carried. Her outfit was canary yellow, and she looked like a breath of spring, presenting a lovely picture as she stood there.

A voice shot out like an arrow from the partially open door at the foot of the stairs.

"Has Chloe left yet?"

It was Anne Lisak, Elise Thornton's sister-in-law and business partner. Elise was Chloe's mother. The two often met in the afternoons, away from the office and ringing telephones, where they could relax with a cup of tea and talk about things besides *Panache*, their wildly popular business that organised fashion shows for charity events. Chloe was brought up short when she heard her name. Of course she came to a halt, listening to the conversation.

"Yes. I believe she has. She was meeting a chap at the pub, to discuss final examinations."

"Elise, I'm absolutely amazed by that girl. She really is going to follow through with her dream of becoming a veterinarian, isn't she? I never thought it would happen, but she has never wavered off course."

"Times have changed, Anne. Young ladies are branching into all sorts of directions. Chloe has loved animals from the time she was a small child. She comes by it honestly, because Sloan and I love them, too. Through the years, our home has been a menagerie. Why, right now, we have four dogs and two cats, not to mention the larger estate animals. So, yes, Chloe will follow through. She's a very bright girl. Actually, she hasn't any more classes. After this, she'll be working in a clinic, doing an internship. Sloan and I are thrilled that she's found something that she loves so much. She'll be marvellous in the field. Chloe has a unique way with animals. She seems to understand them."

"Will her internship be in London, too, just as her university was?" Anne asked.

"Hertfordshire, actually, in a clinic associated with the Royal Veterinary School."

"You must be so proud of her. Do you ever think back to how it all began – with the wretched rape? I still remember when you told me about those despicable Nazi soldiers who attacked you so viciously, resulting in Chloe's conception."

"It would be hard not to ever think about it, but actually I seldom do. Since my marriage to Sloan, and his adoption of Chloe, it's as if those vile creatures never existed. I think of Chloe as Sloan's daughter, and so does he. I've spent twenty-two years of my life protecting Chloe from the knowledge that her father was a Nazi."

"So, she still thinks that her father was a Frenchman who died at Dunkirk?"

"Yes. I suppose someday we'll tell her the truth, but as the years have passed, I wonder why we should do so. Chloe is happy, and I can see nothing to be gained by shocking her with such a revelation."

Chloe stood stock still. Had she heard correctly? *Her father was a Nazi?* How could that possibly be true? She'd always believed her father was French and was killed at Dunkirk before she was born. Later, when she was five years old, her mother had married Sloan Thornton, after their move to Thornton-on-Sea, his family home. Chloe knew she was adopted, but no one had ever said anything about a Nazi. What she'd overheard stunned her. It was hard to take it in. She sank down on the bottom step of the stairway, trying to catch her breath. She was the child of a Nazi? Everything had been a lie? Her bottom lip had gone numb. She reached up and touched it. Shock, she supposed.

She was still sitting there when the door fully opened. Elise and Anne came walking out, still chatting. Anne was leaving. The two women stepped, looking startled. Elise felt dread and fear wash over her body. Chloe had heard. She must have heard. After twenty-two years of secrecy, her most dreaded moment had arrived. Her daughter's eyes met hers. It was clear from their expression that Elise wasn't mistaken. The time for secrets had ended. Thoughts raced through her mind. She needed Anne to leave. She needed to sit down with Chloe and have the talk they should have had long ago. She'd meant to tell her, but life had been so good. There'd never seemed to be an appropriate time. Either Chloe had been too young to understand, or at an age where the truth would have disrupted her life. In truth, Elise had hoped she'd never have to reveal the facts about the day Chloe was conceived. She was a happy, healthy, well-adjusted girl. Why was it necessary to turn her world upside down with the truth about something that nobody could change? Well, none of that mattered now. She'd overheard the conversation. It was the worst possible way for her to have learned the truth. All of it had been so long ago. Elise tried not to show her anguish. She smiled at Chloe, trying to act as if everything were perfectly normal.

"Hello, sweetheart. I thought you'd left. You look so pretty in that yellow. Anne is just about to leave. If you have time, why don't we have a cup of tea together?"

Chloe stared at her mother and didn't answer. Was she in shock? Anne immediately recognised the situation and said that she'd let herself out. After the door closed, Elise sat down on the bottom stair, beside her daughter.

"Chloe. We need to talk. I know you overheard my conversation with Anne. Please come into the library, so that we can be comfortable. I have quite a bit of explaining to do."

"Yes, you do," Chloe murmured in a sullen tone. She slowly rose from her seat on the stairs and followed Elise. The jaunty mood she'd displayed only moments before, while hurrying down the stairway, was gone. In its place was confusion, anger, and disbelief. Once settled in two chairs, facing one another, Elise began to speak.

"Oh, Chloe, I would give everything for you not to have overheard our conversation. Please try to understand why I've never told you this before. It's not something I ever wanted you to know, although I suppose it was your right."

Chloe showed emotion for the first time. "Yes, Mum. I had a right. I had a right to know that I'm the bastard child of a Nazi."

"Please don't say that. You're the daughter of Sloan Thornton. Get that straight in your head. Sloan has been your father since you were five years old. That will never change."

"Except my biological father is apparently some slime who raped you. Who is he?"

Elise put her head in her hands. How could such a beautiful spring day have become a nightmare in a moment's time? She wished she had time to think more clearly. How should she phrase what she had to say? It was so loathsome – so utterly wretched.

"Chloe, I don't know who he was. Will you let me tell you the entire tale? You need to have all of the facts, as unsavoury as they are."

"Yes, by all means tell me all of the facts, Mum. I'm sure it's a very exciting story." Her tone was sarcastic and mocking.

Elise took a deep breath. She waited a moment, looking at her beautiful daughter, sitting with her head bowed, and waiting for words that would shatter her world. Chloe was beautiful. Perhaps even more beautiful than her mother. At twenty-two, she was just becoming the woman she would one day be. Would this information change her from the bright, happy young lady she was now? Her blonde hair was fashioned in a pageboy style. She had beautiful, long-lashed, brown eyes; a pert nose tilted a bit at the end and her lips were a copy of her mother's, full and sensual, with their own pink colour. Even though her flawless appearance was distorted by a shocked, sad expression, she was still spot-on perfect. It was 1963. Twenty-three years had passed since the dreadful day near Bergues France, when Elise had been accosted in her own home, and had later learned she was pregnant. Twenty-three years of living in England and trying to forget; twenty-three years of building a new and better life. Most importantly, it had been seventeen years of marriage to Sloan Thornton, and of his being Chloe's adoptive father. Elise chose her words carefully.

"It was May 1940, my last day in France. Your Uncle Josef had joined the Resistance, and I was left at our farmhouse, trying to decide whether to stay or go. You've heard the story of Dunkirk. Our soldiers were trapped by the German army, and the heroic people of Britain rescued many thousands from the French beaches. It was on that day. That was also the day I met Sloan for the first time. He'd come to my door, injured from a bullet wound, and I'd helped him. I know you've heard us tell that story. After he left, three German soldiers forced their way into the house. They said I'd broken the law by giving aid to a British airman. Of course, that was a lie. The Germans hadn't yet taken control of France. But I didn't know the truth, and it wouldn't have mattered anyway. They assaulted me in the worst way imaginable."

"Oh my god!" Chloe screamed. Tears streamed from her eyes. "So there wasn't just one. There were three! You don't even know which one of them is my father, do you?"

"Your father is Sloan, Chloe. Creating a child doesn't make a man a father."

"Yes, well, I wouldn't be here today if those Nazis hadn't violated you, would I? What does that make them? Sperm donors?"

"Chloe, please. It wasn't something I asked for. It was the worst moment of my life."

"And I've been a reminder of that moment ever since, haven't I?"

"Oh, no. No, Chloe. Never. You were the only beautiful thing to come out of such a sordid experience. God gave you to me as a reward for what I'd endured."

"Oh, Mum, how absurd. Do you really believe that? Or, is that something you accepted as true in order to deny the reality of how revolting the pregnancy must have been?"

"Chloe, I loved you from the beginning. I never associated you with the brutality of that day."

"But I'm the living example of such brutality. You say that Sloan is my father, and yes, legally he is. But would he have chosen that role if it weren't for the fact that he wanted to marry you? I doubt it very much. I was part of the package, wasn't I? What did you tell him? 'Take Chloe, or you don't get me?'"

"Oh god, Chloe. He *wanted* you. He was delighted to have a beautiful little girl. From the moment we married, you were the apple of his eye."

"Perhaps. At least until Reese came along. Do you think I never noticed the difference between how both of you treated your son versus how you treated me?"

Reese Thornton was Sloan and Elise's fourteen-year-old son. He was heir to the Thornton estate and naturally had an uncommon closeness with his father. But Chloe was wrong about Sloan showing favouritism for one child over another. Sloan loved his daughter with every fibre of his being. However, it wasn't unusual for a person in her state of mind to imagine such partiality. Elise knew there would be no use trying to convince her differently. Not when she was in so much emotional turmoil. Elise was glad Reese was still at Eton and didn't know the entire story either.

"Everything is crystal clear now. You and Giselle, living in that cottage with the 'No Regrets' sign outside. What a laugh. You had a *big regret* living right there with you. *Me*. I don't know why you chose to have me. Everyone would have been better off if I'd never been born."

"Chloe, that is absolutely not true. You've been the joy of my life. You still are. Never say such a thing again."

"I won't say it, but I can bloody well think it."

Elise had never heard Chloe use such language. Under normal circumstances, she would have been reprimanded, but this was anything but a normal circumstance.

"Sweetheart, I repeat. None of this was my fault. I tried to do the best thing possible, and I believe that's what I did. Because of you, a sordid experience turned into a gift from God."

"Rubbish, Mum. Rubbish. What a wonderful gift. Did you ever try to find those disgusting, filthy pigs after the war was over? They should have been hanged. What they did was a crime. Even I know that."

"How could I have found them? You have no idea what those times were like. God willing, they were all killed in the war."

"But what if they weren't? What if they're still alive, living perfectly lovely lives? They got away with it. And you did nothing to punish them. I thought Sloan had so much influence. After all, he's an earl. You mean he couldn't have traced those men?"

"Chloe, you've always called him 'daddy'. Why are you now saying his name?"

"Because he isn't my daddy. I'll never call him that again. I'm not trying to punish him. Just the reverse. I'm sure he'll be relieved. Every time I said 'daddy', he must have cringed inwardly. How could he have helped but think about my being the spawn of a Nazi pervert?"

"Oh Chloe, you need to talk with him. Perhaps he can make you understand how deeply he loves you and how wrong you are to believe the way you do."

Chloe stood. "I don't want to talk with anyone. I want to get out of here. I don't belong here."

"You *do* belong here. This is your home. Where are you going?" Elise felt panicky.

"I don't know. Can't you understand that I need time to think? This is an enormous shock. I've just found out that I'm not who I thought I was. I don't know who I am anymore."

"You're the same bright, beautiful young lady you've always been."

"Maybe. Or maybe I have an evil, dark side that just hasn't appeared yet. I'm angry that you never even made an attempt to seek justice. You just let those brutes get on with their lives. Perhaps I'll find them and punish them myself."

"Chloe. Please. You're talking nonsense. It couldn't be done."

"Do you know their names? I suppose not. They were just three animals."

Elise thought for a moment. She *did* know their given names. She would never forget them. But should she tell Chloe? Wasn't it enough to leave things as they were, or was her daughter owed every bit of the truth, after being lied to for so many years? She decided to be completely honest.

"Yes. I do know their names. Well, not their entire names. I only know what they called one another during the awful attack. They were Wolfgang,

Pieter, and Dieter. Those are very common German names, Chloe. They won't do you much good."

"We'll see about that. I have more spunk than you, Mum. I'm not one bit afraid to go after them. I'd like to force them to look me in the eye."

"But... but, what about your schooling? What about your dreams of becoming a veterinarian? Are you going to throw them all away because three filthy Nazis did something evil in 1940?"

"No. I'll take my exams. After that, I'll have the summer free until my internship begins in the autumn. I'll travel to Germany and find the bastards. Somehow I'll find out which one planted the seed that became me. And he will pay. Dearly."

"Chloe, please. I beg of you. You're in no shape to make such a rash decision. Please think. Leave if you must. Go back to your London flat and think. But don't do something you'll regret for the rest of your life."

"Like you did, when you decided to have me?"

Elise was sobbing. "Don't be cruel, Chloe. I've never once regretted my decision. Ask Aunt Violette. She was there. She knows everything that happened. She'll tell you how much I wanted to have you."

Chloe turned and started back up the staircase. "I'm going to pack my suitcase. I'll drive to London. I need to study for my exams. They're the day after tomorrow. Somehow I'll get through them. Thank God, I'm a good student. It's probably due to my German heritage," she added sarcastically.

Elise ignored the barb. "Will you ring and tell us your plans? Please, Chloe."

"Perhaps. But leave me alone. I don't want any more discussion. Don't let Sloan show up wanting to have a chat. The time for a chat is over. Both of you should have been honest with me a long time ago."

2

Sloan came home to find Elise slumped over the arm of the sofa in the drawing room, weeping softly.

"Elise? What's happened? Why are you crying? Come here, sweetheart," he said, putting his arms about her. "Tell me what's wrong."

She sat up and wiped her eyes. Taking a deep breath, she told him everything that had happened, starting with opening the door to the drawing room and finding Chloe sitting on the bottom step of the stairway.

"Sloan. She's devastated and very angry. She's got it into her head that she wasn't wanted and that she's served as a reminder of that awful day in France for her entire life. I tried to argue with her, but she won't listen. She's convinced that the only reason you adopted her was because you wanted to marry me. Sloan, she actually believes that you've only tolerated her all of these years for my sake. You should have heard her saying that both of us treated Reese differently – showed favouritism toward him and that she always noticed it." Elise broke into tears once again.

Sloan reached for her again. "Shhhh. She's distraught, Elise. People always say things they don't mean when they're upset. This was a big shock to her. When she's had more time to think it all over, she'll come to her senses and realise that it isn't true. No parents could ever love a daughter more than we love Chloe."

"I know, Sloan. I tried to tell her that. But I've been thinking ever since she left, and I can understand what might contribute to such feelings. I hate to say it, but Chloe was spoiled unmercifully when she was very small. She was the absolute centre of my universe. In addition, she had Giselle's full attention before she married Ted. There wasn't a whit of competition for affection in Chloe's life. That lasted for five years. Then you came along. She probably would have resented your presence and having to share me with you, except *you* set about spoiling her, too. Let's face it. She was given everything she wanted. All she had to do was ask. We were lucky, because she never acted spoiled. But then two things happened that probably had a huge effect upon her."

"Reese was born," Sloan broke in.

"Yes, Reese was born. But I went to work, too. I went to work for Anne at *Panache* and later became her business partner. A lot of time was devoted to that. Between a new baby and attention to work, Chloe undoubtedly felt a little neglected. She wasn't, of course. Remember, I even made certain my hours were such that I was home before she returned from school. But it doesn't matter. I don't think we thought much about the impact those two events might have had upon her."

"Elise, that's not true. I distinctly remember talking about making certain that we paid extra attention to Chloe when Reese was born. You even bought books on how to introduce a new baby into the household."

"I know. And I don't think we *did* pay less attention to her. But we probably didn't think about was what was going on in her little head. There had to be jealousy and envy when she saw us cuddle and fuss over Reese. Especially for a child who'd been so doted upon. I'm not saying we did anything wrong. I'm only trying to understand what she's going through now. If the truth about the Nazi's hadn't come out, I don't think she'd be saying or thinking such things."

"You're right. Since she's learned the truth, it's caused her to look back and see things that aren't really there – to substantiate a mistaken belief that she wasn't as loved as Reese, and was never wanted."

"Oh, Sloan. What's going to happen? She swears she's going to hunt these men down. I believe she means it."

"Elise, even if she were to find them, what good would it do? How does she think that would make any difference?"

"She thinks they should have been brought to justice. That's one thing she's angry about. Chloe thinks that you, or I, should have turned the world upside down to find them and made certain that they were punished for what they did. She thinks we didn't care enough to do that."

"She has no idea how difficult that would have been. You know, I *did* think about doing that when you told me the awful story. But it seemed better not to make you relive all of the pain again. We were in love and happy. We had Chloe. Our life was good. I figured we'd let God take care of those monsters, and our best revenge would be to live a happy life."

"I know. I did, too. I truly don't know if I could have faced all of the trauma accompanying a search for them. I remember hoping they were all dead, which was, and is, a real possibility."

"Chloe just needs to understand how we felt."

"Sloan. She says she'll never call you 'daddy' again. From now on, she's going to refer to you as Sloan, like you're practically a stranger."

"That's pure rubbish. She's being a bit dramatic. I completely understand how she feels. At least as much as I can. But there's no reason to be angry with me. Nor you. She just feels angry in general and has to direct it at somebody."

"She says she isn't angry at you - that she's trying to take the burden away from you for having to tolerate listening to her call you 'daddy' all of these years. She's got it into her head that every time she said 'daddy', you thought about the Nazi's. Chloe thinks you were repulsed by her."

Sloan put his head in his hands and ran his finger through his hair.

"Oh my god. I can't imagine she honestly believes that. I can't possibly have done anything to make her think that way. I love her so much."

"She knows that, Sloan. Deep in her heart, she has to know that. No child ever had a more loving father. Just as you said, she's twisted everything up in her mind. I just hope she comes to grips with this and works it out. I don't know what we can do to help her."

11

"Well, for starters, I'm going to have a long chat with her. I'm not going to have her muddling about with these ridiculous thoughts. The idea of her trying to conduct some sort of search for those three maniacs is ludicrous, too. The trouble is, Chloe is very, very goal oriented. When she wants something, she goes after it with a vengeance. Look what she's accomplished with her education. Most of her friends from grammar school days are married now, but she's rigidly stuck to her plan to be a veterinarian. She's done it, and she's going to be very successful. I couldn't be more proud of her, but it frightens me to think she might use that same sort of drive to search for, and find, the men who raped you."

"Yes, that's true. But your intent to have a chat with her may be fruitless. She told me not to let you come near her – that she wasn't going to listen to anything you had to say."

"That may be, but I'm going to try. I *am* her father, Elise. No father on earth would sit back and watch this happen and do nothing."

"I understand. I *want* you to talk to her. I just wanted to warn you about her attitude."

"Attitude or no attitude, she's still my daughter, whether she likes it or not."

"Sloan, there's one other thing. What do you think we should do about Reese? He's got to be told the truth, too, now that Chloe knows. She's bound to tell him eventually. Probably sooner rather than later. While it won't be the same sort of shock to him, it will be upsetting. Reese is so level headed and sensible. I can't see him going off on a rant about it, but he's also very honest. I love that about him, and we've always tried to foster that characteristic in both of the children. Now, he'll think we've lied to him all of his life. It's the old 'Do as I say, not as I do.'"

"He *does* need to be told. After I've had a chance to chat with Chloe, which will be tonight, we need to ring Reese at Eton."

There was a pause in their conversation. Both sat in deep thought, mulling over the proper way to handle the entire mess.

"Sloan, let's not ring Reese. The school year is coming to an end. I don't want to interrupt him at this time. He'll be home in a little over two weeks. We'll be able to sit down with him then and discuss it all in depth. If we ring him now, he'll have to come home for a few days and then return to school with this on his mind. We aren't about to tell him the whole, miserable tale on the telephone. We don't need two children in a confused state."

"No. You're right. We'll wait."

Sloan looked at his wristwatch. I need to leave, Elise. If I'm to get to London at a decent hour, I should be on the road now. Please go upstairs and settle down. Crawl into bed. I'll be home as soon as possible. Don't worry about this. I'll chat with her, and try to make her think rationally."

"All right, darling." Elise put her arms around Sloan's neck. They kissed and held one another. "I love you. Drive safely."

⚉

The road from Thornton-on-Sea to London wasn't terribly congested. It never was at that time of night. The worst times of day were early mornings and early evenings, when commuters were slogging their way to and from offices. Since the war, and particularly in the past decade, between 1953 and 1963, masses of people had migrated from the city to more distant towns and villages. The trains ran far more frequently than they had in the past. They were packed during those same hours. Thornton-on-Sea had remained a quaint, quiet hamlet, for the most part, although it hadn't totally escaped growth. The expansion had been good for local business, and nobody complained. Since the town was on the sea, cost of property was quite dear, which meant that the people it attracted were generally professionals. Businesses like Elise's, and her brother-in-law Josef Lisak's, thrived with the increase in population. Both were dependent upon people with a fair amount of discretionary income. Josef owned *Chez Chloe*, the French restaurant named for his beloved niece. Elise's business, *Panache*, a special events service, featuring fashion shows sponsored by charities as fundraisers, thrived on middle-class ladies' ability to afford contributions to worthy causes.

Elise and Sloan had enjoyed a wonderful life together with few bumps in the road since their marriage in 1946. The waters had been choppy before that time, with the war and a love that sometimes looked as if it might not bear up under the strain of outside forces. Elise had endured terrible misfortune, beginning with the rape by the three Nazi soldiers in May 1940. That horrendous ordeal had caused her to immigrate to Brighton, England, where she'd unintentionally landed in a brothel, operated by a French woman named Violette Beaulieu. Thinking it was a boarding house, she'd been guided there by her neighbour in France. As it turned out, Violette was a godsend. Only three months after her escape from the Nazis, Elise had discovered she was pregnant, and with Violette's help and advice, a precious little girl had been born in February 1941. Elise had named her Chloe Arabella, and the baby had become the light of her life. Brighton had also brought good fortune to Elise in the form of her friendship with another French refugee named Giselle Dupris.

The two had teamed up and moved to Thornton-on-Sea, where they'd leased a charming cottage near the sea, and Giselle had found work as a lady's maid at Highcroft Hall, the seat of the Thornton family, headed by Lord Rowan and his wife Lady Celia Thornton. Their son, Sloan, had been engaged to the loveliest girl in the region, Anne Whitfield, daughter of Lord Adrian Whitfield, and his wife, Lady Caroline. They were a Duke and Duchess who lived at Meadowlands, in the village adjoining Thornton-on-Sea, Whitfield Cove. Sloan had met Elise, earlier that same day on which she was later ravaged by the Nazi soldiers, when, as an RAF pilot, his plane had been shot down. His leg had been severely injured, and he'd managed to find his way to her farmhouse. The moment he'd met her, his life had changed. Convinced that she was meant to be his soulmate, he'd broken his engagement to Anne and vowed to find and marry Elise after the war was over. Anne enacted revenge upon both Sloan and Elise, nearly destroying their commitment to one another. However, their love proved stronger than Anne's wrath, and steadfastness won out. Years later, when clearer heads prevailed, Elise became partners with Anne, joining her in the business Anne had started.

As Sloan drove through the lonely night, he thought back on all of the years he and Elise had shared. He'd adored Chloe even before they'd married, and the moment he was able to, Sloan had legally made her his daughter. He'd bought her a pony and taught to ride; together they had explored every stretch of land on the Thornton estate; he'd bought her two puppies, and romped with them on the lawn, nurturing her fledgling passion for animals; they'd read stories by the fire in the library, and he'd taught her the names of every county in England; together they'd memorised the long line of monarchs in English history. He'd taught her prayers and listened to them every night at bedtime. Later, he'd waited anxiously for her to return from her first date with a chap from Whitfield Cove. Sloan remembered how proud he'd felt when he watched her presented to the Queen and danced the first dance at her debutante ball. It didn't seem possible that he was now on his way to London to convince her that he loved her with all of his heart.

He'd known this day would come. At least, he'd known she would someday have to be told the truth about what had happened to her mother on that tragic day in May 1940. But it had always seemed like it was too soon, or simply not the right time. It wasn't the right time now, but it had happened. It had happened, and he was no more prepared to explain everything to her than he had been when she was five years old. He only knew that he was her daddy and had to try. He wasn't going to lose her now.

3

Chloe drove her little car to London, as she'd done countless times before. But never had she been so muddled and confused. She vacillated between sorrow and anger, and occasionally burst into tears. When she finally arrived in the city and had parked the car, she quickly entered her flat by the front doorway. The forward-facing garden was already beginning to bloom. It was such a beautiful setting, and it was difficult to feel downhearted.

Chloe had always been blessed with a wonderful ability to wall off unpleasant things in her world, if she needed to concentrate on something important. This was one of those times. Her examinations, for the end of the academic year, were around the corner. Her entire career in veterinary medicine hung in the balance. Always an excellent student, she had no intention of falling apart at the end and throwing away years of study and work. She had only been home for the weekend to study for the exams. Normally, she lived in her rented London flat, near the university. It had already been let to a new tenant, as of the following week, when exams would be over. She was due in Hemel Hempstead in September to begin interning at the university clinic.

She'd been moving her belongings back home when she'd overheard the conversation between her mother and Anne. Taking a huge breath, she told herself that no matter how upset and shocked she was, nothing was going to interfere with her lifelong plans. She would push the revelation of her Nazi paternity out of her mind and focus on her studies. Once that was over, she'd concentrate on seeking justice for her mother and herself. Whatever she'd undertaken in life, she'd always done well. It was conceivable that she would move heaven and earth to find the wretched scoundrels and make certain they paid for what they'd done. Chloe was a sweet natured, kind young lady, but when roused to anger, or pushed too far, she could become stubborn and vengeful. This was one of those times.

She hauled her textbooks and notebooks into the flat and dumped them on her desk. Her first task was to prepare as thoroughly as needed to pass her exams with flying colours. No Nazi pigs were going to rob her of her dreams. She settled down to study, stopping only once to eat a sandwich and an apple. After about three hours, she heard the sound of a car door slamming in front of the building. She didn't need to wonder who it was. Of course it would be her father – or Sloan, as she now intended to refer to him. Sure enough, there was a sharp rap on the door. Chloe got up and opened it.

Sloan stood on the step, his hair mussed, as if he'd been running his fingers through it, as he was prone to do when upset. He was such an astonishingly handsome man, and Chloe had always been so proud to call him daddy. But she couldn't do so now. He wasn't her father, and she firmly believed that he'd probably never wanted to be. He'd accepted her reluctantly, because she came as a package with her mother. Well, he'd performed his duty, and Chloe intended to remove the burden.

"Hello, Sloan. I told Mummy that I didn't want to see you, so why are you here?" Chloe asked, coldly. It was hard to maintain such a façade.

"All right, Chloe. We'll have no more of this. I understand you've had a terrible shock. We probably should have told you all of this long before now. But that doesn't mean we should be crucified for our poor decisions. Your mother is terribly upset. So am I."

Sloan didn't wait for an invitation. He simply walked into the living area, closing the door behind him.

"Now, young lady. We are going to have a chat, whether you like it or not. My heart aches for you. I know this was a terrible way to learn the truth, but that's no reason to hurt your mother – or me, for that matter. Everything we've ever done in our lives has been with your happiness in mind. If we were less than truthful, it was because we could see nothing positive resulting from revealing the repugnant details of Elise's ordeal. It appears to me that because you're shocked and angry you need to take it out on someone, and your mother and I are the logical candidates. But that isn't fair, Chloe. We love you with all of our hearts. I am as much your father as any man on earth. I've earned the right to be called 'daddy'. I've been there for you every step of the way."

He wandered into the parlour, and sat down by the fireplace. Chloe followed, still not saying a word. After several more moments, she finally spoke.

"Yes, you have been," Chloe answered. "But I wonder if you would have been, if you hadn't fallen in love with my mother. You were forced to take me on, if you wanted to marry her."

"Rubbish. I took you on, as you put it, because I wanted to. I loved you then, and I still do, a hundred-fold more. Do you think I'd have done all I have for you, if you'd been a burden?"

"Yes. For my mother. To please her."

"Chloe, this is idiocy. Your mother tells me that you're now accusing us of showing favouritism to Reese after he was born. Nothing could be further from the truth. Parents can love two children. Reese was a baby. He needed our full attention for a spell. You were so used to being the only child, I'm sure it was hard to share us at first. But, you know Reese thinks you hung the moon, and until now I thought you adored him."

"Reese hasn't anything to do with this, except that he makes it easier for you. You have your heir to the Thornton fortune, and you've done your bit for me."

"Why are you so blasted angry with me?"

"Because you let them get away with it. You didn't lift a finger to find the creatures and see them brought to justice. Was she really raped? Or was it consensual? Is that why you never looked for and prosecuted them?"

Sloan briskly walked across to Chloe and slapped her face. He had never before laid a hand on her, but the comment was over-the-top. He was shaking with anger. Chloe's hand flew up to her cheek. The slap hadn't been very hard, and she was shocked more than hurt. She began to weep. Sloan took her into his arms and patted her on the back.

"I'm sorry, Chloe. But I cannot let you say such things about your mother. That was unforgivable. Upset or not, there will be no derogatory statements made about Elise. She could have done away with you. She could have given you up for adoption. Instead, she choose to give you life, without the faintest notion of how she'd support you. She was alone and frightened. It took great courage to do what she did. Don't ever make that sort of remark again."

Chloe hung her head and sobbed harder. Sloan held her closer. "Chloe. I'm sorry. I've never laid a hand on you in anger in my life. But, to suggest such a thing about your mother won't be tolerated. She the finest woman in the world."

Chloe wiped her eyes again. "Sorry. I shouldn't have said that. I'm all in a muddle. I feel very angry and don't know who to strike out at."

"That's understandable. But try to remember that we did the best we could. Don't you think I'd love to have found the buggers? But, Chloe, it would have been impossible. You have no idea what the world was like. Now, Elise tells me you have some nonsensical idea of finding them yourself. That's an insane idea. It could even be dangerous. You know nothing of Germany. You don't speak the language. There are probably thousands of men with the same names. Where would you begin? They could well be dead by now."

"They should be, if they aren't."

"I agree. But that isn't up to you."

"Oh, don't fret. I'm not going to murder anyone. At least I don't think so. But if I find them, I'll turn them into the authorities. They committed war crimes. I want to ruin whatever lives they have left."

"Oh, my dear. Revenge doesn't become you. You're going to waste precious time in your life. The best revenge is to live your life well. Don't let their evil acts affect all that you can be. And, anyway, Chloe, I *did* do some investigating, long ago. The Statute of Limitations for such crimes is past."

"Oh, wonderful. So nothing at all will happen to them. They ravaged a poor, innocent girl and faced no repercussions."

"Chloe, our family believes in a higher power. I don't think they'll escape retribution. Let God take care of it. Continue with your plans and be happy."

"That's easy for you to say. You aren't the spawn of the devil."

"Chloe, please. Neither are you. You're forgetting that you're also your mother's child and have all of her kind gentleness. Look at your love of animals. That came straight from your mother. Can't you concentrate upon that?"

"Yes, and I shall. I can do both. Once the scoundrels have paid for their actions, I'll be ready to focus all of my attention on my career."

"Is there nothing I can do to change your mind?"

"No, nothing."

"Then what are your plans?"

"I'm going to sit for my exams on Monday. Then the new tenant will take over my flat here. I'm not certain from there. I need to do some thinking. I have a plan, but it isn't completely formulated yet."

"Will you share it with me?"

"No. Because you'll try to stop me."

"Chloe, I realise you are not a child, but you've had a bad shock. Do you think it's wise to be making plans under these circumstances? Perhaps a few days of rest at home would be good for you."

"No. That's the last place that would be good for me. I need to get away. I need to feel like I'm doing something to bring those savages to justice."

"Will you at least stay in touch? Let us know where you are, and what you're doing? Chloe, we're worried."

"No need to worry. I'm not a child."

"Have you enough money?"

"Quite enough, thank you. My trust fund has scarcely been touched."

Sloan had established a fund for her so that she was financially independent when she turned twenty-one. It gave her a substantial income every year.

"I don't intend to squander it, if you're worried about that. It will be used for a good purpose. I probably should return it to you. If I thought it was a hardship for you to provide for me, I would do it. However, since it's going to cost money for me to do what you and Mum should have done long ago, I think it's fair that you should have to pay my expenses."

"Chloe, don't talk nonsense. I'm not worried about the money, and I'd never let you return it. I'm worried about you. All I can do is beg you not to do anything foolish. If you *are* going to Germany, I wish you wouldn't go alone."

"I can't think of a soul who'd go with me. But, I'll think about it."

Sloan looked at her with penetrating eyes. "Chloe. I adore you and always have. If something happened to you, it would break both of our hearts. Please remember that. We are always here if you need us. Just ring, and I'll come to you wherever you are."

"It's time I settled things on my own. This really isn't your fight."

"Anything that concerns you is my fight. I'll come with you, if you want me to."

"No. I don't want you with me. I want to meet them on my own. Not like some little girl, whose daddy has come along to protect her."

"*Am* I still your daddy, Chloe? I certainly think of myself that way."

"I don't know, Sloan. You're the only father I've ever known. But I have to do this. Can't you understand? Wouldn't you want to know who'd given you life?"

"I can't say, Chloe. I don't know how I'd feel. But if that's the way *you* feel, I'm not going to stand in your way. Just promise you'll be very, very careful, and that you'll keep in touch."

"All right. I do promise that. I feel numb at the moment. I know what you're saying, but I also know what I feel. There's still a part of me that believes you took on the job of fatherhood because you felt you had no choice. I have to work those feelings out. Right now, I feel like all of my memories of a daddy were a sham of some sort."

Sloan felt like he'd been stabbed in the heart. He stood silent for a moment. Then, he gave her a kiss on the cheek and held her closely. Chloe didn't move a muscle and kept her arms stiffly at her side. Sloan shook his head sadly, sighed deeply, turned around and left the flat. He had to go, for fear that he would burst into tears. What she'd said had wounded him to the core.

Chloe knew she'd hurt him and didn't know why. She wasn't being herself. Everything in life seemed like a giant lie. Perhaps it wouldn't have been so bad if she'd found out that her mother had been married before, and that there was a living father somewhere. A ne'er do well of some sort, perhaps. But, no. This was entirely different. *Three Nazis.* Why didn't her mother kill them? Chloe would have killed all of them. Instead, her mother, figuratively, let them kill her. They robbed her of her innocence; took away her pride and dignity; planted a child in her womb and walked away to live their lives, leaving her to fend for herself like a wounded animal.

Chloe definitely meant to find them, no matter what. They had to look her in the eye and know what their jolly moment of drunken fun had wrought.

4

After exams were over, Chloe cleared out all personal items from the flat and loaded them into her car. Over the past three days she'd decided on a plan of action. Her mother had mentioned Aunt Violette, the wonderful lady in Brighton, with whom her mother had lived after her escape from France. If it hadn't been for her, Chloe might never have been born. Violette was now married to a nobleman – a wonderful gent by the name of Lord Tom Sterling, a baronet from Somerset. Thus, Violette was Lady Sterling. They lived in a gracious old mansion. Violette had been like a mother to Elise and like a grandmother to Chloe. Early on, Chloe had called her Auntie Violette, and the name had stuck. She loved her as if she were truly a member of the family. So the first place Chloe thought to go, when she'd had time to think it all through carefully, was *Coeur Jolie*, the Sterling's lovely estate

Violette had adored the Sterling family home from the moment she laid eyes upon it, and the name had guaranteed her acceptance of Lord Sterling's proposal of marriage. *Coeur Jolie* meant 'happy heart' in French, and because Violette was originally from France, she might have named the house herself. Yet, it dated far beyond its present occupants, having been built in the 1500s, by a Frenchman named Nigel de Sternai. Through the centuries, the name had been anglicised to Sterling. Chloe had visited there during summers, after her mother married Sloan Thornton, and Violette married Lord Tom Sterling. The marriage had been a wonderfully happy surprise. Violette had operated a bordello in Brighton, since the early 1930s. She was a highly successful Madam. She'd never dreamed that an aristocratic member of the gentry would want to have anything to do with her, after learning how she earned a living. But, no. Lord Tom had not been upset, or even annoyed with Violette. All he'd wanted to know was how much the business earned in a year, and when he heard that the figure was substantial, he proposed to Violette on the spot. So, they had married. Violette was now Lady Sterling, and they were both very happy. Violette still owned the brothel, Maison de Violette, but had promoted one of her best girls to run it for her. Lord Tom had been in full agreement.

And so, Coeur Jolie was like a second home to Chloe. The mansion sat outside of the village of Sterling-Mendip. The Mendip Hills are a range of limestone hills to the south of Bristol and Bath, and Chloe adored that part of England. She could walk for miles, enjoying the incredible views of lovely meadowland interspersed with breath-taking knolls. She knew Violette loved her. There was no question about that. She was the best person Chloe could think of to listen to her plight and offer sensible, unbiased advice. She drove her car in the direction of Somerset, wondering if she should ring Violette to let her know she was coming. After much deliberation, Chloe decided she would simply arrive at Violette's door. From what she remembered, Lord Sterling's grandson was also in residence. His father, Roger Sterling, Tom's son, had died in the war, leaving Sheppard, Lord Tom's only grandson, heir to the Sterling title, mansion, and fortune.

She knew he'd graduated from Oxford and had done the Grand Tour. Chloe had never cared for him much. Like most chaps of his ilk, he was a bit full of himself and had no use for an adopted daughter of another member of the nobility. However, it didn't matter a whit what Sheppard Sterling thought of her. She wasn't paying *him* a visit. It was Violette with whom she wished to speak – Violette who would give her sound advice and honesty. Sheppard was living there to be groomed for his eventual takeover of *Coeur Jolie*. Perhaps Chloe wouldn't have much contact with him. At least she hoped not.

Coeur Jolie was one of the finest examples of Elizabethan architecture in Great Britain. Set in over nine hundred acres of parkland, with over six thousand acres of woods and farmland, it also claimed a true safari park, just like those found in Africa. Nothing could have been more thrilling to Chloe, the girl who loved animals' almost more than anything else in the world. She'd spent hours watching the various species of exotic creatures that roamed freely in the magnificent setting. In addition, the family had several domestic animals of varying species. As a matter of fact, it was that aspect of *Coeur Jolie* that most drew Chloe to the Sterling's home and always had.

It was late afternoon when she turned her car into the gravelled drive leading to *Coeur Jolie*. She came to a stop in front and briskly walked to the massive entry door, after disengaging from the auto. The butler, Davison, answered the door. He knew Chloe well and was delighted to see her. She quickly found herself in the Elizabethan great hall, complete with a minstrels' gallery. Chloe was always awestruck at its beauty and expanse. She was shown to the Blue Library, which had a display of over forty thousand books and a hand-painted Venetian ceiling. It was Chloe's favourite room in the splendid home. Tea was immediately brought to her, and it was only a short time before Violette arrived to greet her. Taking both of the young girl's hands in her own, Violette kissed her on both cheeks.

"My darling Chloe. What a happy, unexpected surprise. I'm so pleased to see you. What brings you to *Coeur Jolie?*"

Violette motioned for her to sit, and then chose a place next to her on the down-filled sofa.

"How perfectly splendid to see you. You're looking even more beautiful than you did the last time I saw you. When was that, now? Lands sake! It's been over a year. Have you finished your studies?"

"I've finished the classroom portion, Auntie Violette. All that remains is my internship, which will be done at a clinic run by London University at Hemel Hempstead. I've a break till then. I will begin work in the autumn."

"So, have you come to spend the summer with us? We'd love it, you know."

Violette was as spry as ever, although she was now nearing her sixtieth year. She still dressed in her signature colour – various shades of purple. One never saw her in anything other than a frock of lilac, lavender, grape, orchid, or heather. Her jewels were always amethysts. Her white hair was arranged to perfection, and her choices brought out the colour of her eyes, which were so blue that they looked violet. There was nothing intimidating about her. She was the sort of person whom one felt they could cuddle upon meeting.

Chloe answered her question. "No, not for the summer, although I wish that were true. I can think of nothing I'd like better. But, I'm going through a rough patch, and you're the first person I thought about."

"A rough patch? But my darling Chloe, what sort of rough patch would you be experiencing? Is it to do with university? Or a young man?"

"No. Neither. University is going well. I'm graduating with top honours. There is no one special in my life, and that's the way I've wanted it. There are lots of friends, but no one chap I'm truly interested in. I want to finish my studies first."

"Then what the devil is causing you consternation? More importantly, what can I do to help?"

Chloe leaned back against the cushions on the sofa and began to tell her tale. Of course, there wasn't one part of it that Violette didn't already know. She'd sheltered Elise upon her arrival in Brighton, after the Nazi soldiers had assaulted her. It was Violette to whom Elise had gone when she first suspected pregnancy, and Violette who had been with her every step of the way until Chloe was born. However, even though she knew the details of the trauma intimately, she listened quietly as Chloe recited what she'd learned. After reaching a stopping point, when tears began to fall, Violette took the young girl in her arms.

"Oh, my poor darling. What a wretched way to learn all of this. How can I help?"

"Tell me, Auntie Violette. You were there. Tell me if my mother *really* did want me, or if she kept me out of guilt? Do you believe that Sloan wanted me, or did he just give in and accept me as his daughter because he wanted to marry Mummy? And why didn't anyone go after the horrible men who did this thing? Why weren't they prosecuted? Everyone seems to have just let them get away with having perpetuated the most evil of all acts."

"Chloe, I assume you've already spoken with your parents about this?"

"Yes, of course. But I'm not sure what I should believe. After all, they've lied to me all of my life."

"Chloe, I wouldn't phrase it that way. They did what they thought was best. I think they always planned on telling you, but the time never seemed proper. You were such a happy, well-adjusted child and young lady. It seemed cruel to interrupt your life with information that made no difference in the long run."

"Oh, but that's where you're wrong. It *does* make a difference. Don't you think everyone has a right to know who they are? I've been sailing through life thinking my father was a Frenchman who was killed at Dunkirk while Mum was pregnant. I've always believed that I was the daughter of a French hero. Instead, I'm the bastard child of a Nazi!"

"You are the legal daughter of Lord Sloan Thornton, one of the finest men I know. Aren't you forgetting that, Chloe?"

"Perhaps. I have a lot to sort out. I question whether Sloan really loves me like a daughter. He'd do anything for Mum. But I *have* noticed a difference between the way he treats Reese, and the way he treats me."

"Rubbish. I was around during the days you were growing up – much younger than Reese is now. No father ever doted on a child more. Of course he loves Reese, too. It's an entirely different set of circumstances. Reese is his son and his heir. They'll always have that special bond. But that certainly doesn't mean Sloan loves you any the less. You must get that idea out of your head."

"And what of Mum? She must have been shocked when she learned about me? How could someone want the child of a rapist? And it wasn't only one man. It's loathsome."

"Many women probably wouldn't have. But your mother is one of a kind. From the very beginning, although she was frightened and confused, she never once wanted anything other than to make you happy. She made the decision that you would need her and that she would need you, too. You were the be-all and end-all. She loved you with every fibre of her being. She still does."

"Did she only marry Sloan to get a father for me?"

"Absolutely not. Elise would never have married at all. She wasn't even thinking along those lines. As you can imagine, she had very little trust in men. Her plans were to raise you alone. She wanted to give you the best life possible, and believe me, she would have, Sloan or no Sloan. Chloe, isn't there any way you can put all of this behind you? Yes, it was a terrible thing. Particularly terrible for your mother. But she managed, and you've grown into a daughter anyone would be proud of. Who cares about what happened to those filthy men? The one thing we know for certain is that they never got the joy of seeing you, or knowing that out of their despicable brutality came a beautiful young lady. It was their loss, not yours."

"But, Auntie Violette, I need to know *who I am*. I simply have to. Half of me comes from one of those 'filthy men', as you yourself put it. I cannot go through life not knowing who he is – if there is any resemblance to me. I can't live knowing that none of them were ever punished for the evil they did. I want to look them in the eye and tell them that they are the scum of the earth."

There was silence for several moments. Violette and Chloe both sipped their tea, and the clock on the mantle chimed the half-hour. Finally, Violette spoke.

"I understand how you feel, Chloe. I suspect I, too, would feel the same way. But assuming that were true, how on earth would you ever find those swine?"

"I've thought and thought about that. I think I've come up with a way. I shall place an advertisement – a rather large one – in several newspapers, starting with the ones in France, in villages throughout the region where the farm was located. In those advertisements, I'll give their first names, which I know, and offer a reward to anyone who has information about them. I need their full names, where they were from, and the like. There may still be someone who knew them while living in the region. If that doesn't bring results, I'll go farther afield. If necessary, I'll place large advertisements in every single German newspaper, asking for the same information. The word 'Reward' can be very enticing. I won't give any indication that I want to see them for any nefarious reason. Many, many people are still trying to locate people they met, or knew, during the war. I'll also scour any official documents. It's possible I can find names from there. I don't necessarily expect that the three who attacked Mummy will come forth – reward or no reward. But I believe it's possible that there is someone out there who knows who they are. That's all I need to know. If I can find out their full names, and where they originated, I'll track them down."

"And then what?" asked Violette.

"Then, I'll decide. First, I want to see them. To talk to each one. I want to find out which one is my biological father, if at all possible. I want them all to pay a price for what they did. I won't be satisfied until I feel like I've vindicated Mum and myself."

"All right, Chloe. Let's assume you go on this quest. I absolutely do not want you to go alone. You know nothing of Germany, and I'm not going to shoulder the responsibility of having you trek off to a place where we Englanders are probably still not well liked. You're a remarkably attractive girl. Anything could happen to you."

"I can take care of myself, Auntie Violette."

"No. You do not know that, Chloe. I'll have no part of this scheme, unless you promise to take someone with you."

"Who… who on earth would want to spend a summer in Germany, searching for three rapists?"

"I'll speak to Sheppard."

"Sheppard? Your husband's grandson? I scarcely know him. And frankly, Auntie Violette, I don't really like him. I don't think he likes me either."

"No matter. You don't have to like each other. You have to protect one another. He's here at *Coeur Jolie* now. I'm sure Tom can let him go for the summer months. I won't speak any more about this unless you agree to have him accompany you."

"Oh, all right, Auntie Violette. I think it's silly. But I suppose it can't hurt. I'll have to sit down and go over all of this with him."

"Yes. He'll be here for dinner. He's out with Tom now, watching the stable master train some horses. I'll talk to him when he returns, and let him know that the two of you have an appointment to chat after dinner."

In the afternoon, Chloe spent time looking through countless books in the *Coeur Jolie* library, searching for names of newspapers where she was most likely to place advertisements. Then she spent quite a long while working on the proper wording for her campaign. She wrote it in English, but naturally, it would appear in whichever language was appropriate to the locale where it ran.

ATTENTION!

SUBSTANTIAL REWARD AVAILABLE!

Three German soldiers, who were in the vicinity of Bergues, France on May 10, 1940, are being sought. This is not a police investigation. It is essential that their full names be revealed, as well as their native cities or towns. The three travelled together and are described as follows:

Light haired, fair skinned, muscular build. Their given names were Dieter, Wolfgang, and Pieter. They were not officers, although could later have been promoted to officer ranks. They may have been based in or around Bergues. If you have any information regarding these men, please contact:

Lord Sheppard Sterling,

C/O Coeur Jolie Abbey

Sterling Mendip

Somerset, England

The advertisement would be run in all newspapers in and around Bergues, France. If necessary, a duplicate, written in German, would appear in every city newspaper in Germany. It would cost a fortune, but Chloe wasn't to be deterred. She couldn't think of a better way to spend some of her trust money. Sheppard's name would be used as a contact, since Violette and Lord Sterling were adamant that Chloe's name would appear nowhere. A gentleman's name leant more creditability to the inquiry anyway. Chloe studied the map of Germany for hours. She wanted to learn where each and every place was located. She wouldn't be traveling to Germany in the initial phase of the search. Not yet. The idea was to run the advertisement and wait at *Coeur Jolie* to see what sort of response it brought. Hopefully it would be productive. From there, the decision would be made about which, if any, replies to take seriously. After that, she would decide where to travel.

Chloe became more and more excited as she made plans. There wasn't a doubt in her mind that she would find the three Nazis who had invaded her mother's home, forever changing her life and planting the seed that one day became Chloe herself. Although her parents thought she could never find the brutes, Chloe knew better. When she set her mind to something, she seldom failed. Even if they were dead by now, she wanted to visit their graves and speak out loud the hatred she held in her heart.

She completed her research in the library at *Coeur Jolie* shortly before it was time for the dinner gong. Racing up the stairway, she ran a quick bath, and changed into a lovely pink cotton sundress, trimmed with eyelets on the shoulder straps and hemline. Lord Tom and Violette did not dress formally for dinner, which was good because Chloe hadn't brought a lot of fancy clothing. She had one evening gown, but everything else consisted of frocks with cardigans, or trousers and blouses. It was summer, 1963, and the day had arrived when women wore trousers more and more – not simply for riding or sporting events. One still never wore them on any sort of dressy occasion like church, or even shopping in London, but they were acceptable for wearing at home and leisure-wear. She brushed her long, blonde hair and refreshed her lipstick. It was time to chat with Sheppard Sterling and convince him that the plan was viable. The idea of having to embark on any sort of trip with him was not pleasant to contemplate, but if that's what it would take to accomplish her goal, then she'd buck up and tolerate him as best she could. Deep in her heart she *did* feel better about not having to go through the ordeal alone.

Once downstairs, she made her way to the drawing room, where several bottles of liquor sat on a chest against one wall. She selected a glass, poured some tonic water, and added a measure of gin. A squeeze of fresh lime completed the drink. Then she wandered about the room, admiring the various odds and ends adorning the tables. Violette was a collector, and her style of decorating was quite Victorian, so most of the surfaces were filled with silver-framed photographs and precious crystal items. There was one particular collection of Lalique crystal animals that Chloe adored. Someday, she promised herself, she would have such a collection in her own house, since her life was going to be revolve around four-legged creatures. As she stood examining the precious items, a male voice interrupted her thoughts.

"Well, if it isn't my old nemesis, Chloe Thornton. I must say, you're looking almost beautiful. You've actually developed a bust line. Quite a nice one, actually. How long has it been, old thing? At least two years, I'd wager. Perhaps more."

"I've missed your back-handed compliments, Sheppard," answered Chloe, without even turning around. "It's been nearly four years. You were at

Oxford, and I'd just started at the University of London. You laughed at my ambitions."

"Yes, well, who wouldn't have? Not many girls choose veterinary medicine as a career. But I hear you've finished the course work. So, I suppose it's time for me to eat crow. Congratulations, Lady Thornton. Well done."

Chloe turned to face him. She was surprised at Sheppard's appearance. The last time they'd met, he had spots covering most of his face. There'd been nothing remotely attractive about him. His hair had been reddish brown, and eyes a faded blue. Back then, he'd been rather awkward and thin. He had worn a sweatshirt that said Oxford on the chest, and it had looked like it was badly in need of a wash..

Now, however, there had been an amazing change. His hair had darkened quite substantially, and he wore it longer, combed to the side in front. He'd filled out and had nice shoulders and arms. The eyes were sparkling blue and his skin was smooth and clear. He had marvellous colouring - lovely, very pink cheeks – typically English. She wondered if the improvement was due to contact lenses. Most importantly, he'd learned to dress like a gentleman. He wore what was quite clearly a Savile Row suit, with a crisp white shirt, school tie, and expensive loafers. She suspected Gucci. The difference, as a whole, was startling.

Of course, he was equally taken aback. The skinny young lady he'd remembered was now a ravishing beauty. She, too, had filled out, in all of the right places. He was sorry he'd made such fun of her. Teasing was really the only way he'd known how to relate to the opposite sex in those days. His personality was still such that he was given to sarcastic banter and a ribbing sort of repartee. But Chloe was able to give as good as she got, so their conversations had always consisted of taunting, making fun, mocking, and badgering. Shep could never quite tell if Chloe was being honest in some of her derogatory comments, or if it was just her way of relating, as it was his. Nonetheless, she'd developed into a stunner.

His step-grandmother, Violette, had told him a little about the mission Chloe wanted to undertake, searching for the man who was her biological father. She'd asked if Sheppard would accompany her, to keep Chloe from harm and to be there if she needed a shoulder to cry on. Sheppard hadn't been at all keen about the idea, but now that he'd had a look at Chloe, those feelings radically changed. He couldn't think of anything more enjoyable than spending an entire summer with such a stunning creature. Chloe had similar feelings. Although she expected Sheppard's attitude hadn't undergone a transformation, he was a lot more pleasant to look at, and that would make time spent with him less annoying. Actually, their joking with one another, and teasing, had always been a bit of a lark. He kept Chloe on her toes.

Sheppard mixed himself a drink and sat down by the fireplace on the sofa. Patting the seat next to him, he motioned for Chloe to sit down beside him. She ambled over to where he sat and sank down onto the soft couch.

"So, tell me about this mission you want me to undertake," he began.

"It's dead serious, Sheppard. I intend to find the dirty swine who attacked my mother back in May 1940, which resulted in my birth. There were three of them – Nazi soldiers. Her little farmhouse was near the town of Bergues, France, not far from the Dunkirk beaches, which is how she managed to escape to England. I've no idea what became of the brutes. I suppose they could be dead by now. But I mean to find out."

"That's a tall order, little Miss Detective. What do you know about finding long-lost people?"

"Not a blasted thing. But I have a good brain. I can learn. My first plan is to place an advertisement in several newspapers. I'll start in France." Chloe reached over and picked up the notebook she'd been working with all day. She showed him the facsimile of the advertisement she'd drawn up.

"Not bad. I see you've used my name. Didn't think to ask me, did you?"

"Oh Sheppard, don't be obtuse. Of course I was going to ask you. I was just mucking about. Auntie Violette had already said she wanted me to use your name in the adverts. If you don't like the idea, we can change it."

"No. I'm just pulling your leg. It's fine. Actually, I like the advert. It should attract attention. The word 'Reward', always does. This is going to cost a pretty penny. Do you have the funds?"

"Of course I have the funds. I know what I'm about. Don't worry, I'm not going to ask for any of your money."

"Didn't think you would. I'm supportive only to a point, old thing."

"Please stop calling me old thing. I hate it."

"What would you prefer?" he smiled.

"Just Chloe."

"Too formal. I'll call you Cuz."

"But we're not cousins. Actually, we're not related at all. Auntie Violette isn't really my aunt, and your grandfather is no relation whatever to me."

"Well, you know I tend to nicknames. So you'd better decide what I'm to call you. You can call me Shep."

"Shep sounds like a dog."

"That's all right. You love dogs, don't you? I wouldn't mind being your dog."

"You aren't special enough to be my dog," she laughed.

"I know. I'll call you Pip. I once had a dog named Pip. She was small and sassy, so it fits."

Chloe sighed. "That's better than 'old thing'."

So, it was settled. Pip and Shep would put together plans to travel over half the continent, if necessary, to find the thugs who'd committed such an evil act.

5

Sloan and Elise received a call from Violette Sterling a week after Sloan's visit to London. There had been no word from Chloe, and they had been nearly frantic with worry. Thus, when the call came, both breathed a tremendous sigh of relief. At least they knew where their daughter was and what her plans entailed. They had to admit, between themselves, that her decision to go to Violette had been an intelligent one. Violette was one of the most sensible, clear-headed people they knew. And perhaps most importantly, Chloe was much more likely to listen to what she said than she was to her parents. At least at such a precarious time. They also had to admit that Chloe's plan to run advertisements was a practical one. She wasn't directly running off to Germany – at least not yet. But apparently that was definitely the ultimate goal, and it sent shivers down both of her parents' spines.

Chloe didn't have her mother's memory of that horrible, rainy day in 1940. She didn't remember how strong and large the men were and how totally devoid of feeling. The thought of her adored daughter coming upon them frightened her. Elise closed her eyes and tried to picture them. She'd blocked so much out of her mind. Even at the time, she was only half aware, having willed herself to step outside of her body – to separate herself from the pain and degradation. She remembered they were all blonde, with very short hair, like all of the military men wore. She thought all of their eyes were blue, but she wasn't even certain of that. She'd been twisting her head from side to side and sobbing throughout the ordeal, so she didn't recall their eyes ever having met. She thought she would have remembered if that had happened. In her memory one of them might have been somewhat kinder than the others, but that may have been her imagination, too. Perhaps kinder wasn't the proper word. He seemed more reticent. He was the last one, so it was probably the knowledge that the nightmare was approaching its end that made him seem less like a beast. Her memory had to be faulty, at best. She couldn't even have described their uniforms, except for the hated Nazi Swastika. And the pants they were wearing had buttons. She remembered that.

She actually hoped Chloe wouldn't be able to find any of them. It would be far better if they'd all died in the war. Chloe could be like a dog with a bone when she set her mind to something, and Elise knew her daughter wouldn't stop until she was satisfied that they were dead, or she'd found them. The only good part about this supposed trip to Germany was Violette having set down the rule that her grandson, Sheppard, must accompany Chloe. Elise couldn't help but smile. She was well aware that Chloe loathed the young man. At least Elise and Sloan wouldn't have to worry about Chloe going off on this journey with a member of the opposite sex and falling madly in love. Their daughter had always shown amazing good sense when it came to matters of the heart. Perhaps because of her passionate goal to complete veterinary college, she hadn't had time for young men. She'd met heaps of them, since her college was predominantly male. There had only been one other female student in the veterinary program. Because Chloe was such a lovely creature, there had been no shortage of interest in her. But she'd had a wonderful way of making it clear that she wasn't interested in any sort of romantic liaison, yet still managed to keep a chap's friendship. As a result, she was very popular and had scads of young male friends. In an era when the rules had been greatly relaxed, Elise and Sloan were grateful for their good luck. There was no question in their minds that Chloe was still innocent when it came to sexual matters, and they hoped to keep it that way until she decided to marry. Taking Shep along on the proposed trip didn't have the potential to sabotage their expectations. Chloe had never given the slightest indication that he interested her. Elise remembered that he was an underweight, rather anemic looking young man. Of course, it had been nearly four years since she'd seen him. He'd probably changed a lot.

Violette promised to keep them informed as plans moved forward. It was made abundantly clear that Chloe should not know of the contact between Violette and the Thorntons. Such a breach would cause Chloe to lose all trust in Violette, and Sloan and Elise's one line of communication could be closed. They wondered about speaking to Sheppard, but Violette thought it wasn't a good idea. He just might slip at some point and let the cat out of the bag that her parents were being kept abreast of their moves. Then Chloe wouldn't even trust Sheppard, let alone Violette. It was imperative that she trust Sheppard. So, as difficult as it was, Elise and Sloan had to sit back and wait for the occasional call from Violette. It was very, very difficult.

In the meantime, there was Reese to contend with. He was returning from Eton for summer break in two days' time. At least there had been an interval when they'd been able to think about how they intended to tell their son everything that had happened. Of course the most difficult part, was revealing to him that Chloe was the child of a Nazi, and about how that had come to be. Though he was just a fourteen-year-old boy, he was mature for his age. Sloan had always treated him as the heir to his family's title and estate, and the boy had taken it seriously. He was a typical youngster, of course, and not a miniature estate manager, but both of his parents felt they could rely on his common sense and stable way of looking at things. He was not a hysterical child. Still, what they had to tell him was bound to come as a huge surprise. He had always known that Chloe was his half-sister, but, just like her, he had always assumed that her father had been a Frenchman, killed at Dunkirk and married to Elise.

Sloan and Elise tossed and turned and spoke of little else in preparation for his homecoming. The conversation had to be handled in just the proper way. Their biggest fear was some sort of scene with Reese. Chloe was enough for them to deal with at the moment. Reese adored Chloe – always had, from the moment he was old enough to recognise her face peeking at him in his baby cot. His first smile was for her. He was sure to be upset by anything that had wounded his sister.

Finally, the day arrived. They were collecting him at the Thornton-on-Sea station at two o'clock in the afternoon. Elise and Sloan were there early. They'd discussed driving to Eton to bring him home, but then decided that any change of plans would seem strange to him. He'd been riding the train alone since he was twelve. All of the other boys were allowed to do the same, and Reese wouldn't have liked it if they had suddenly told him they were coming over to get him. He was at the age where boys wanted their independence.

As the train pulled into the depot, they looked up and down the carriages, hoping for a glimpse of his face. Finally they spotted him with a gaggle of other boys just descending the steps of a car. Every time they saw him, after a spell away at school, they were amazed at the change. Even more so now. At fourteen, he was changing almost overnight. He was no longer the little boy Elise had loved to cuddle in her arms. He'd sprouted up a lot and could have passed for a young man of sixteen. He was going to be a very attractive man. At the moment, he was still gangly and a little like an overgrown puppy, but there was a tremendous resemblance to his father. Because Sloan was such a handsome chap, Elise was thrilled that her son would take after him. There was a faint resemblance to Elise too, but he was clearly a Thornton. Sloan's parents had worshipped him, and both Elise and Sloan had been so pleased that the elder Thorntons had lived long enough to not only see Reese as a tiny baby, but to have known him as a young boy. It was important to Sloan that Reese have memories of those two adored people. Lord Rowan and Lady Celia had died within a year of one another, as often happens when two people have been together for a good part of their lifetime. He had died first from heart difficulties, and she had followed with a stroke. They lay side by side in the family cemetery next to the chapel, which was attached to the house by a cloistered walkway. Sloan had been devastated at their loss, and the full weight of responsibility for Highcroft Hall had been thrust upon him. But Lord Rowan had prepared him well, and the transition couldn't have been any smoother. Similarly, from the moment they'd married, Lady Celia had groomed Elise to take over the duties of countess, and Elise had done so seamlessly. For a farm girl, born in Russia and raised in France, she performed her duties as well as any English aristocrat. Sloan was tremendously proud of her.

Young Reese walked calmly to where his parents stood. It would never have done, of course, to show too much enthusiasm about seeing them. After all, his friends were watching. Elise and Sloan were circumspect in their hugs, being careful not to be overly effusive. Sloan did throw his arm about his son's shoulder, and that seemed to suit Reese perfectly well. They ambled to the car where Gerald, the family chauffeur, took the boy's bags and stowed them in the boot. Elise was surprised that her son's first words of greeting were "You're looking lovely, Mum." It was a quite an unexpected accolade. In fact, she couldn't remember his ever having given her a compliment before. She spontaneously blushed. Of course she *did* look lovely, clad in a pink Chanel suit, with a cerise blouse peeking out from the jacket. Her pretty blonde waves tumbled to her shoulders. Not many boys his age had such striking mothers, and Reese was well aware of it. He was vastly proud of both of his parents.

They chatted on the way home, mostly about school, and what he planned to do over the summer. That entailed a long list of things he wanted to accomplish at Highcroft Hall. Just as Lord Rowan had done with his son, Sloan was grooming Reese to someday become the earl. It was important that it be done correctly. There were fewer and fewer large estates in England. Ever since the Great War, which had ended in 1918, and then the Second World War, it had become more and more difficult to maintain such large properties. Many had been sold off; others were demolished; still more opened their doors to the public to raise funds for taxes and upkeep. Sloan didn't want any of those things to happen to his beloved ancestral home. He had already made Reese well aware of the enormous responsibilities that would be his someday.

They entered the house through the rear door and Mrs. Littleton was there to greet Reese. She had seen two generations of Thornton boys off to Eton and was past the age where she should have taken her pension, but she continued on, a bit less spry but as capable as ever. Reese adored her, just as she did him. After a more demonstrative show of affection than he'd given his parents, Reese raced up the back staircase, shouting that he was going to change from his school uniform and wouldn't put it on again until autumn. Elise and Sloan looked at each other and laughed. Some things never changed at all.

When he returned, they asked him to join them in the drawing room for three o'clock tea. The three settled themselves comfortably, and tea was poured. There were scones with lemon curd, chocolate fancies and various cakes. Reese tucked in, like a starving animal. After a few brief remarks, Sloan took a breath and decided it was time to launch into the subject that had occupied his mind for days. Before he had a chance to speak however, Reese asked, "Where's Chloe? I thought she'd be home by now. Weren't her exams over last week?"

Sloan cleared his throat. "Yes, they were. She's gone over to Violette and Tom Sterling's for a spell."

"What's she doing over there? I thought she'd want to see me when I got home."

"I'm sure she does, but something unexpected came up. We want to discuss it with you."

"Something unexpected? What's that? Nothing unexpected ever happens around here."

"Well, something has," smiled Sloan. "It's a bit of a tale, but you need to hear it. We think you're definitely old enough to understand how it all came about."

"What in blazes are you talking about? How what all came about?"

"Reese, you've always known that technically Chloe is your half sibling."

"You've never called her that before. Nobody has. Are you barking mad? Chloe is my sister. That's it. My sister. What are you talking about? I don't think of her as my 'half' sibling, or whatever you're saying?"

"Well, none of us do, Reese. But, you remember that she was five years old when I married your mother. I adopted her, and she became Chloe Thornton. Of course she's your sister. That's the way we've always thought of her and always will. That's why I said she is 'technically' your half-sibling. Simply because I am not her biological father."

"So What? So, Mum was married before you. That happened a lot during the war, didn't it? Women got married and had babies, and then their husbands were killed. So, when that happened, women got married to another person."

"Yes. That did happen a lot. That's what we let Chloe think until now. We wanted her to be old enough to understand everything."

"What are you saying, Dad? Do you mean you lied to her all this time? And to me too?"

"We waited until you were both old enough to handle the truth."

"Well then, what is the truth? Did Mum have Chloe without being married?"

"Yes. But, it wasn't the way you're thinking. She was an innocent girl, and three Nazi soldiers attacked her. Do you understand what I'm saying?"

"Course I do, Dad. That's revolting. That's just plain disgusting. You mean Chloe is one of their children?"

"Yes, Son, that's what I mean."

"Egad, Mum. I can't stand the thought of you having to go through something like that. How did you stand it? The buggers. They should have been shot." Tears were beginning to fall down Reese's face, which had lost all semblance of being grown up and reverted to that of a small boy. "What happened to them? I hope they were shot, or hanged, or whatever they did in those days."

"None of those things, Reese. No one knew about it. Your mother was in shock when they left her, and she did the smart thing. She escaped to England. This happened in France, on the day of the British evacuation from Dunkirk."

"They were never reported? They just got away with it, scot-free?"

"It was a chaotic time. If Mum had stayed and reported it, she may not have escaped the Nazi occupation of France. There is no guarantee anything would have been done to the monsters anyway. She did the right thing."

"I suppose so. I wish someone had been there to help her. I wish I'd been there. I'd have killed the bloody bastards."

"Reese, watch your language. I know you're upset. It's an upsetting bit of news. But it happened a long time ago. Chloe is twenty-two now. She's had a wonderful life, and so has Mum."

"Yes, Reese, I have. Your father is right. I *did* do the right thing. I escaped to England and freedom. I was fortunate and met good people. They helped me, and I had Chloe. I was mad for her from the beginning. No matter how she came to be. She was my little girl, and just as I loved you from the moment you were born, I felt the same way about Chloe."

"Didn't she remind you of what those men did to you?"

"No. Never. I thought of her as a gift from God. I still do."

"So, does it bother you that you aren't Chloe's father, Dad?"

"There's where you're wrong, Reese. It isn't very hard to make a baby. Men who shouldn't, do it all of the time. But, it's extremely hard to be a father. I've been a father to Chloe from the day I married your mother. When I adopted her, I became her legal father. Don't ever think of me as not being Chloe's father. Just as I don't want you to think of her as not being your sister. She is."

"So, how does Chloe feel about all of this? I'll bet she's pretty upset. Is that why she's with the Sterling's?"

"Yes. It was her decision to go there. Your Mum and I are glad she did. She needed time to think. They're sensible, caring people, and she's in good hands."

"Is she angry?"

"She's sorting out her feelings. She says she's going to find the men who did this to Mum and make them pay for it."

"That's my sister! I'll be surprised if she doesn't do it. Can I go and help her, Dad?"

"Under no circumstances, Reese. We're not at all happy about her plans. They're foolish, reckless and could be dangerous. We're not *allowing* this. There just isn't any way we can stop it. At least Violette has managed to get her to agree to let her grandson, Sheppard, go with her."

"That creep. He won't be any help. I could help a lot more."

"Reese, that's unkind and uncalled for. Sheppard is a decent, young man. Just like you, he'll be taking over Tom and Violette's property someday. He's level headed. That's what's called for."

"That may be, but I don't like him. I never have."

"You scarcely know him. I believe the last time you saw him, you were ten years old."

"That's old enough to know if you like someone or not."

"Reese. It doesn't matter if you like him. He's the one who is going with Chloe. Stop arguing."

Reese stopped talking, but it was clear that his mind hadn't been changed.

"Look, Son, we know this is a lot for you to absorb. Don't worry yourself about what Chloe is going to do. Mum and I don't intend to let anything bad happen to her. We just want to make certain that you know and understand the situation. I'm not sure that you should tell Chloe you know about it. Let her be the one to come to you. As close as you've always been, I can't imagine that she won't. But you can make up your own mind. I'm not ordering you to keep quiet about what you know. You're not a little boy. I just want you to think carefully. Chloe has been handed a huge shock. She's not thinking straight about a lot of things right now. I don't want you to be hurt, or to hurt her further, by something completely innocent that you might say or do. Do you understand?"

"Yes. I understand. I need to think about all of this, too. It's a pretty unbelievable situation."

6

The advertisements were placed in all of the newspapers. They ran on a Sunday morning, in prominent type, in all of the largest towns closest to Bergues. If Chloe and Shep didn't get any response from these advertisements, they would branch out to larger French cities. But common sense dictated that if the three men had been assigned to a village, town, or province near the Lisak farm, where Elise and her brother, Josef, had lived, someone in that vicinity would have knowledge of them. Often the Nazis who were assigned to oversee certain areas remained there throughout the war until France was liberated in 1944.

The two young people waited a full week. A few letters arrived at *Coeur Jolie* referencing the advertisement, but none contained the information they hoped for. One interesting note asked that if the men were located, the writer would be most grateful to have their names, since she was quite certain they were the same three who'd perpetrated crimes upon her own family, near Bergues. Shep wrote down the name and address of the woman who'd penned the letter, with plans to speak with her at a later date. They were about to give up and ring other newspapers and to place the same advertisement, when a very intriguing letter arrived. It was the one they'd been looking for. It was, of course, written in French, but after translation, it read as follows:

"Dear Lord Sterling;

I am writing with regard to the advertisement you recently posted in the Roubaix newspaper. I would prefer, at this time, to remain anonymous. I believe I know the three men whom you reference. Their names are Pieter Schoen, Wolfgang Wilt, and Dieter Schwab. All three assisted in low-level positions in the village government during the days of occupation. They were despised. The eldest was Pieter, and the youngest was Wolfgang. Wolfgang seemed to hold great sway with the other two. It is my understanding that all three came from the same village in Germany, a place named Klasse, in Hesse-Darmstadt. I have no idea what became of them after France was liberated. After D-Day they would have been sent to fight. Wolfgang left before the others. He was disciplined in some manner. One would assume they returned to their home village. I hope my information might be of some use to you. If it should result in your finding these three men, I would be interested in the reward. Should that be the case, please place another advertisement in my newspaper, and I shall respond. God bless you, and be safe. These men were evil.

Sincerely,

An Interested Party

Chloe was beside herself. In only one week, they had discovered the full names of the wretched Nazis and now knew their origin. She immediately ran to the library and found a map of Germany. The town was located in the central part of Germany near the Rhine River. Hesse-Darmstadt was the region where the village of Klasse was located. She and Shep had learned that Sloan was right. The Statute of Limitations for crimes such as rape of French women had already expired, so if the men were to pay for what they'd done, it would have to be at the hands of their young, English avengers. Neither had the foggiest notion what they would do when, and if, they found the heartless beasts, but both felt they would know when the time came.

Shep had thrown himself full force into the search. At first, it sounded like fantasy on Chloe's part, but once the letter arrived, his attitude abruptly shifted. He was more than eager to start their trip to Germany.

"Pip, I have it figured out. We'll fly to Frankfurt and take the train to Klasse. Klasse looks like a small village, so we'll have to be careful. If they're still living, we can't just barge into the town and start asking questions. We'd surely arouse suspicion. We'll have to go about this very carefully."

"Shep, I wasn't born yesterday. Of course we'll have to be careful. If you think I intend to come this far, only to fail, you're daft. I wish I could speak German. It would be an immense help."

"I can speak it quite well. Not perfectly, of course. Any native would know I'm a foreigner. But I *did* study it at Oxford. I think it's an ugly language. I only learned it because we had to read German philosophers in their native tongue. I'm pretty rusty."

"That's better than nothing. At least you'll be able to read road signs and directions. Can you drive in Germany?"

"Of course. Do you think I'm a dolt?"

"Do you really want the answer to that?" Chloe smiled, slyly.

"Never mind, Pip. Just be glad you'll have my help."

"Oh, Shep, I'm on my knees every night, thanking God that I have you in my life," she laughed sarcastically.

"You are one cheeky, little, smart-arse. I don't know how I ever got caught up in all of this."

"Yes, you do. You're secretly madly in love with me and jumped at the chance to be my protector."

"Oh ho! Protecting you will be like protecting a wild rabbit. I expect you to go running off on your own with no warning."

"That's a distinct possibility. Don't think I intend to wait for you if I need to be someplace and you're lagging behind."

"Seriously, Pip, we have to stick together. No going off on our own."

"Oh, all right. I suppose that's why we're together after all."

At Violette's insistence, Chloe rang her parents. She told them where she was and went on to explain about the response they'd had from their newspaper advertisements. Both Elise and Sloan were surprised at the headway they'd already made. They were glad that Chloe sounded so encouraged, but were also worried about the next part of the plan. They hated the idea of Chloe going to Germany in search of the men. But, nothing they could have said or done would have made the slightest difference. Sloan even begged her to come home and promised he would make arrangements to have a detective take over. That didn't satisfy Chloe at all. She was adamant that she would look them in the eye herself. So, in the end, all Elise and Sloan could do was tell her that they would be praying for her, and ask her to keep them informed. Sloan literally begged her to ring him if she actually was able to find where the three were living. Chloe said she would do so.

But secretly she wasn't at all certain that she really would. It was *her* task. She didn't need her adoptive father intervening. She was still having a lot of difficulty accepting that Sloan truly cared about her as a daughter. In her heart, she felt that if he hadn't needed to adopt Chloe in order to marry Elise, he would never have done so Everything had happened so quickly, and while on the surface Chloe seemed determined and resolute, a part of her was still in shock over what she'd learned. Rationally, she understood why the truth had been kept from her, but emotionally, it had taken its toll. She held on to some deep-seated anger at both of her parents for lying to her about who she was. There was no question in her mind that if she hadn't overheard the conversation between her mother and Anne Lisak, she still wouldn't know the truth. It seemed hard for people like Violette, and even Shep, to understand why it was so important for her to know the truth, but they weren't the ones who were walking around not knowing half of their identity. Chloe was the sort of person who needed the entire picture. That was why medicine had been so interesting to her. It had logic, and there was completion. One found symptoms, causes and treatments. Then the problem was, hopefully, resolved one way or another. There was that element of detective work in her chosen field. One searched until one had answers. That was what she intended to do in the current dilemma.

There was more discussion between Chloe and Shep about whether or not to place a separate advertisement in the Klasse newspaper. Shep was in favour of doing so. Chloe wasn't so sure. What if the men saw the advertisement and decided to leave town? Might they become suspicious that it could relate to their unsavoury activity during the war? Chloe and Shep finally decided to make the trip to Klasse and very tentatively ask around. They would begin by checking telephone listings and continue from there. A local library often had a lot information.

So the trip was planned. Chloe was glad that she had packed her passport. She would not need to return home for it, and have to face her parents trying to talk her out of going to Germany. Airline tickets were arranged from London to Frankfurt. From there, a train would take them to the village of Klasse in Hesse-Darmstadt. After finding out whatever they could in Klasse, they would then decide how to continue with their quest.

Violette and Lord Tom took them to Heathrow, where they boarded a Royal United Kingdom Flight to Frankfurt. Chloe had never flown before, and it was an exciting experience. Shep was more blasé about it, but Tom and Violette had insisted upon first-class tickets, and that part was exhilarating. As a student, he'd been used to small seats and not such wonderful food service. But, first class was just as its name implied. Wonderful food and as much wine as one could drink. When they arrived in Frankfurt, both were a bit tipsy. They had reservations at a nice hotel. After collecting their luggage and negotiating customs, they checked into their rooms, which were adjacent to one another. Shep made several comments about how they might have saved on the cost of accommodations by doubling up, but Chloe smirked at him and said she'd rather sleep with a homeless dog. Shep laughed uproariously.

"At least I don't have fleas, Pip," he retorted.

"Yes, but God knows what else?" Chloe shot back.

"All right, Pip. You'll never know what you're missing."

"I have a fairly good idea. Thanks all the same, but I'd prefer a good book and a train schedule."

They laughed, touched cheeks, and retired to their own bedrooms. Chloe was tired, but also filled with excitement. She sat up until the wee hours studying a map of Germany, in particular Klasse. It was not a very large town, with a population of perhaps twenty thousand inhabitants. Chloe thought they were unlikely to find all three of the men still living there. In fact, she was sceptical about finding any of them. Jobs would not have been plentiful, and the town must have been even smaller when the war ended in 1945. Still, it was a beginning.

The next morning they boarded the train and arrived in Klasse by early afternoon. It was a very pretty place, surrounded by forestland and small lakes. Neither Shep nor Chloe could imagine what sort of work one might do in such a place. Once again, they went to an Inn and registered. Because they didn't intend to be there overnight, they asked for only one room. It was a twin bedded, chalet-type accommodation, neat and clean, but nothing fancy. It met their needs.

Once inside, with the door closed, they got right to work. A telephone directory was brought out, and they began to search through the names. Wilt, Schoen, and Schwab. Unfortunately, these were common names in Germany, and the directory had many. There was only one listing that looked like a possibility. The name was listed as D. Schwab. Chloe thought it was a longshot, but Shep thought they should try it. Shep dialled the number and thumbed through his book *'Beginning German'*. The telephone rang three times, and a man answered. Shep launched into his prepared German.

"Hello. My name is Sheppard Sterling, and I am an Englishman. I am searching for a man by the name of Dieter Schwab. He is supposed to have been from this town and was based near Bergues, France during the war. Would this be the correct number?"

The voice at the other end of the phone sounded perplexed.

"Dieter does not live with me. I am his son, David. He is not able to live in a private home. He was gravely wounded in the war. Since his return, many years ago, he has lived at the Home for Soldiers. It is a sort of convalescent home. I wish I could care for him, but it would be very hard. He is nearing forty years old now. Before you would visit him, I should like to meet you first, please."

"Yes. Certainly. I'm here with my friend. We would be very happy to meet anytime, at your convenience."

"Do you have my address?"

"Yes, sir, we do."

"Then, I suggest you take the taxi cab to my home. I shall be waiting for you, and we will talk."

Chloe was concerned about what they would say to Dieter's son.

"Shep, we can't just barge into this man's home and tell him that we think his father is a rapist. How in the world are we going to go about this? I do want to meet him. And, of course, his father. After all, he could be *my* father. But I have no desire to hurt the son. So how do we approach this?"

"We'll stay as close to the truth as possible, without using the word rape. We'll try to learn when the son was born and if Dieter was married when he was in France. He said his father is nearing forty. That would mean that he was about eighteen years old back then. I wish your mother was here to confirm that."

"I don't think she would even know. She wasn't looking at them to try to determine ages. I'd guess they were quite young. She said they were drunk. I think they were probably foolish boys on a lark."

"Well, let's go and meet this David. Don't be nasty to him. Whatever his father did, it wasn't his son's fault."

"Don't be an idiot, Shep. I'm not going to say anything out of line. The chap may be my half-brother."

"'Egad! I didn't think of that. Perhaps you should greet him with 'Hallo, *Bruder*.'"

"I don't think so, Shep." Chloe couldn't help but giggle at the thought.

And so, they were off to meet David Schwab. Arriving at the door to his modest cottage some ten minutes later, it was opened by a well-built, nice looking German chap. He had brown hair and a full face, with a closely shaven beard.

"Welcome. You didn't have any problem finding my home?"

"No. None whatsoever. It was very nice of you to invite us on such short notice," answered Shep.

He introduced Chloe, and reintroduced himself. David Schwab took them into a small sitting area, and offered coffee. Both declined.

"All right, so how can I help you?" he began.

"Well, you see Herr Schwab, my friend's mother thinks she knew your father during the war." Shep pointed to Chloe. "May we ask you a few questions?"

"Yes, certainly."

"Was your father married during the war?"

"I was an orphan. I lost both of my parents early in the war. I was adopted in late 1940 by Dieter and his wife. Later, my adoptive mother died."

"Did your adoptive father have any biological children?"

"No. My father could not have children. He had the mumps disease when he was a young man. It rendered him incapable . . . well . . . you know what I mean."

"Yes. He couldn't conceive children."

"That's correct."

"That answers one of our questions. Let me explain. Chloe's mother was intimate with a German soldier named Dieter Schwab in May 1940. Following that, the Dunkirk evacuation began, and she escaped from France to England. Later she learned that she was pregnant. She thought the baby might have been Dieter's."

"Oh no, it could not have been. There must have been someone else." It was a rather rude statement, but nobody could argue its accuracy.

"You see, your father wasn't alone. He was accompanied by friends. I don't wish to upset you. But, Chloe wants very much to learn who her father is."

"Are you implying that this woman was assaulted?"

"Yes, sir, I'm afraid she was."

"That could not have been my father. Never."

"Do the names Wolfgang Wilt or Pieter Schoen mean anything to you?"

"Yes. They were comrades of my father. All came from this village. They were childhood friends. They were in the Hitler Youth together and then joined the military at the same time."

"Yes. That's what we suspected. There may be a mistake. Perhaps your father wasn't one of her attackers. It's not our wish to cast aspersions on your father. But we would like very much to meet him. It's possible that he could clear up a lot of the confusion."

"I have no argument with you seeing him. It is his decision. He is a grown man, many times over. I shall call the home and speak with him. If he agrees to see you, you may go there directly."

"Thank you so much, David. You've been a great help. Would you like us to leave, while you ring him?"

"No. That will be fine. I'll make the call from my kitchen."

David stood and went through a swinging door, into what was, presumably, the kitchen area. They could hear his voice, but not his words. Shep and Chloe didn't say a word to one another while he was gone. Both drummed their fingers on the top of the table sitting in front of the divan.

After a few minutes had passed, David Schwab returned to the room.

"My father says you are welcome to visit him. I didn't tell him your accusations about the attack on a French woman. I leave that up to you. I find it hard to believe, but then, it was wartime, and he was very young. Men do foolish things at times like that. If he did something like that, he has paid for it dearly."

Chloe and Shep thanked him and left the house with directions on how to reach the convalescent home. They walked a few blocks and found an empty taxicab. Sliding into the back seat, they gave the driver the name of the home, and he immediately knew where to go.

7

The taxi let them out in front of a long, low building, constructed in the 1940s. They entered and immediately came to a reception desk. The place seemed clean enough on the surface, but there was an odour of bleach mixed with urine. They asked to see Dieter Schwab. A girl in a white nurse's uniform came out from behind the desk and led them down a long hallway. Near the end, they stopped at a room where the door was closed. She rapped twice and a voice answered, "Come in." Chloe and Shep walked into the room.

It was arranged like a typical hospital room, with a single bed, side table, one large chair and one straight-backed chair. They were both appalled when they saw the man in the bed. He had no legs. Upon closer examination, he had only one arm. His face was badly scarred, and his hair appeared to have been burned off. It was extremely hard to look at him. Yet, it would have been the height of rudeness to turn their heads away. He was propped up on a pillow. His eyes found theirs, and Shep enquired as to whether he spoke English. They were relieved to learn that he did.

"My son said that you wished to see me. I don't have many visitors, as you can imagine. I was surprised that anyone remembered me. Who are you?"

Chloe spoke first. "It isn't that *we* remember you, Herr Schwab. But my mother thinks she met you during the war."

"Your mother? What is her name?"

"Her name was Elise Lisak. She lived on a farm near Bergues, France. She met you in May 1940. It was near the beaches at Dunkirk."

The man got a strange look on his face. There was no question that he remembered. He heaved a sigh and looked up again. "Yes. I remember that day. It wasn't the proudest moment of my life. I've often wondered if she might find me."

"No, sir. I can imagine it wasn't," Chloe replied. "Yes, she certainly remembers you."

"So, you're her daughter? Were you born before or after that day?"

"After, sir. Nine months after."

"Oh my god. One of us impregnated her. It can't have been me. Did my son explain that he's adopted, and I'm unable to have children? I always have been."

"Yes, he told us that. But I wanted to speak to you because I'm trying to find the man who *is* my biological father. You were with two other soldiers that day, if I understand correctly."

"Yes, I was. Pieter and Wolfgang. We were very drunk. Young, drunk, and very, very stupid."

"Can you explain what happened," asked Chloe.

"We had been drinking Schnapps since noon. By then, it was late in the day. There was chaos all around. People were trying to seek refuge out of France. The English soldiers were retreating to the Dunkirk Beaches. There was no order. The Luftwaffe were strafing the beaches and the roads. I was with my two friends. We'd been together since the beginning, and on that particular day we felt invincible. Because everywhere there was confusion, we had no fear of being discovered by a German officer. We saw an American airman leave a small farmhouse, and the woman who stood on the porch, bidding him farewell, was very beautiful. As young men will do, we got ideas into our heads about her. I would never have acted on them if we hadn't been drinking. Of course, if we hadn't been fellow soldiers encouraging each other, it might not have happened. In any event, it was the perfect prescription for disaster. We crashed into her house, threatened her, and well, apparently you know the rest. I'm ashamed of what I did. We could have been hanged The way things turned out for me, I wish I had been. That was the last woman I ever touched. I've often thought that God brought disaster upon me because of that day. Later, while assisting the officers in overseeing Bergues and that region, I was engaged in combat with a Resistance fighter. I caught him trying to blow up a rail ammunition depot. He threw a grenade at me, and you have the result in front of you. Unfortunately, I was saved. So, you may report back to your mother that I have paid a heavy price for what I did that day."

"I'm sorry, Herr Schwab. But my mother paid a price as well. She was only a young girl, very much alone and terribly frightened. Learning that she was pregnant, after such a horrific experience, was almost more than she could bear."

"Yes. Believe me, I'm not proud of our behaviour. Your mother. How is she now?"

"She is well. She was fortunate to find good people who helped her. She's married now, to a good man who accepted me as his daughter."

"He must be a good man. You're a lovely girl. I wish I could claim you as mine, but that would be impossible."

"What can you tell me about the other two men?"

"Wolfgang and Pieter? They were as different as night and day. Actually, Pieter and I were the better friends. We'd known each other the longest. Wolfgang came from our village, and we knew who he was, but he had a bad reputation and we weren't *besten freudne*."

"I'm sorry. What does that mean?" asked Chloe.

"I believe you English say 'best friends', or 'close to each other'."

"Yes, I understand. What sort of a bad reputation did he have?"

"Wild. Mean. Strange beliefs. He had no heart. I remember that when he was a small boy, he killed animals just for fun."

Chloe cringed.

"He was that sort. Liked to see things suffer. Liked to inflict pain. To tell the truth, he frightened me. He frightened Pieter, too. We talked about it. That's probably one reason we didn't argue about going into your mother's house that day. If Wolfgang wanted to do something, one didn't say no. After that day, I didn't see much of him. I stayed away from him as much as possible. He was discharged from the military. I'm sure it was a dishonourable discharge. No one was sorry to see him go. Pieter, on the other hand, was truly a good man. From that day forward, he never stopped talking about the sin we had committed. It wore heavily on him. Again, if it hadn't been for Wolf, I know Pieter would never have participated. I don't mean to sound like I'm making excuses. We knew that what we were doing was evil and wrong. But our judgment was very poor, and there always has to be a leader in a situation like that, doesn't there? I hope he's dead now."

"That was my next question," said Chloe. "Do you know where we could find either of these men?"

"I think they went to Munich. I'm quite certain about Pieter. Somewhere, I heard that Wolf was there, too. His father had a lot of money. If Wolf is alive, he would probably be wealthy, although many of my countrymen lost everything during the war. So who knows? I'd like to see Pieter again. If you find him, tell him where I am. Give him my address. But if Wolf is alive, don't tell him anything about me. I'm still afraid of him."

"If you were looking for either of them, how would you go about it?"

"I suppose there are official records somewhere. But knowing the government, it would take years. I would probably go to Munich and start there. Just as you found me, I would search the telephone directory. If it helps, Pieter's second name is Richard. I don't know if Wolf had a second name. His father's name was Karl. He was rather old when Wolf went into the military. I would check newspaper obituaries to see if you find his death. Since he was wealthy, I should think it would have been reported. He was a prominent businessman. The obituary might give the son's whereabouts."

"And his mother?" asked Shep.

"Wolf never spoke about his mother. He acted as though he were ashamed of her. I don't know why, but I suspect she might have been Jewish. If so, he would have despised her. He was a fanatic about Jews."

"How strange. Since he would be part Jewish himself," mused Chloe.

"Yes. But then, they say Hitler may have been, too, you know. Who can understand? Wolf was filled with hatred for everyone. It wouldn't really have mattered."

"My god, I hope he isn't my father."

"Miss Thornton, I hope that, too. If you want my advice, I would drop this quest of yours, and go home to England. The war is over and has been for a long while. From what you say, you have a father who was willing to give you his name and love you, in spite of the fact that you are a Nazi's child. He must be a special man. Can't you leave it there? Sometimes it is better not to know things."

"I understand what you're saying. But I have a burning need to know. I don't believe justice was ever done."

"Oh my dear girl. I have no doubt that each of us has paid in his own way. I certainly know that I have. I suspect Pieter has suffered greatly for his actions. As for Wolf, I don't think there is anything that would cause him to suffer. Perhaps finding out that your mother has had a good life. That's all I can imagine."

"He has to be a monster."

"Yes. I wouldn't argue with that."

Chloe was surprised that she felt no anger toward the pitiful man in the bed. He was right when he said he had paid for what he'd done. It was hard to imagine this broken man committing such an atrocity upon her mother. Yet, of course he had. When she thought of that act, it repulsed her. She'd vowed she would spit in all of their faces, but her determination was gone. In its place was deep sorrow, for the young man he must have been – the dreams he must have had – the hopes for a happy future. All lost, because he'd been caught up in the lunacy of Nazism and the carnage that followed. There was silence in the room. It was awkward, and no one really knew how to bring the conversation to a close. Finally, Dieter spoke.

"Miss Thornton. I have no right to ask this. But my mind would rest far easier if I thought your mother might find be able to find it in her heart to forgive me. I'm dreadfully sorry for what I did to her. That's not the sort of man I am, and I'd never done anything like it before. There's nothing I can do to make up for it. I do try not to feel bitterness or anger because of the way my life turned out. I did this to myself, and deserve it. Her forgiveness would bring me so much peace."

"Herr Schwab, I can't speak for my mother, but I will tell you that she is probably the sweetest, kindest lady you could ever meet. I cannot imagine that she'd withhold her forgiveness. I've never even heard her say anything nasty about the three men who assaulted her. I'll take your message to her. I think you can expect a letter in return. Life is so odd. I truly believe that under different circumstances, you would have been fond of my mother, and she would have liked you."

Dieter had tears in his eyes, and so did Chloe. "Thank you for meeting with us and telling us what you know. If it helps at all, I can tell you that I forgive what you did. You have many years ahead of you, and I hope you find a way to make them profitable. I believe you could be a good example to others about the folly of war. God allowed you to live. I hope you're a believer. If so, then you must know that there is a purpose in your life."

"God bless you, Chloe Thornton. I hope you find what you're searching for," he smiled.

———

Chloe and Shep left the convalescent home, subdued and downcast. She'd thought she'd be happy to find each of the men, but she hadn't reckoned on what she would discover about them. Certainly Dieter Schwab had paid dearly for the mistakes he'd made. Chloe's problems seemed minimal after seeing the pathetic sight of Dieter. Perhaps he was right. Perhaps she should let it go. Then a fragment of a poem by Alfred, Lord Tennyson popped into her head; *"to strive, to seek, to find, but not to yield."* It perfectly described how she felt. She wasn't going to yield. She'd come this far. Just because one of the men stirred pity in her heart, didn't mean they all would. She still had the need to know. Once she did, perhaps she could lay the matter to rest.

They found a taxi and returned to the train station. Studying the Departures Board, they found several trains scheduled for travel to the southern part of Germany, which would take them to Munich. Since it was the third largest city in the country, public transportation was plentiful. Chloe and Shep debated about whether to take one of the trains, or to rent a car and drive to their destination. Since they weren't familiar with the roads, and had heard that driving on the autobahn could be treacherous, they decided on the train. They settled on an express route that would deposit them in Munich in eight hours. Shep paid for two first-class tickets, which gave them the comfort of a private compartment, as well as access to the dining car. The train would leave in under an hour. During that time, they wandered the station, buying maps and travel guides for Munich. Between eating, sleeping and reading, the trip would pass quickly.

They boarded as soon as they could and settled themselves for the journey. Shep had regained his jolly mood and was once again bantering with Chloe.

"Well, Pip, upward and onward. I don't suppose I could convince you that continuing on to the Italian Alps would be a more enjoyable trip? How about Lake Como? Or Maggiore?"

They were two of the loveliest areas in the Italian Alps. People travelled great distances to vacation there.

"Shep. Do you really think I'd trust you in Italy? I suppose you've studied Italian too. I have to admit that Italian does things to me that no other language could."

"Yes. I've studied it. I'd have to brush up, but give me a few hours, and I'll be fluent enough to woo you in an outdoor café overlooking the lake."

"Not good enough, Shep. I want the real thing in Italy. Your hair isn't dark enough, she laughed."

"I could dye it."

"Not the same. Your blue eyes would give you away. Face it, Shep. You're not the smouldering, Mediterranean type. My trip to Italy will have to wait. After I'm a full-fledged veterinarian, perhaps I can attend a conference in Rome. I imagine I could find a gorgeous, Roman man, or perhaps a Venetian," Chloe smiled, teasingly.

"You may be right. But, I wouldn't mind meeting a voluptuous Italian lady – perhaps even Sophia Loren"

"Ha! You think a dazzling, Italian woman like her would be interested in you? Shep Sterling, you're daft."

"A man can dream."

Chloe laughed again. She turned to him, and spoke seriously.

"Shep, honestly. Thanks for coming with me on this trip. I thought I knew what to expect, but I didn't. I can't imagine having done this alone. You've made it so much more bearable."

"At your service. It's my contention that even this sort of adventure can be made bearable, if one adds a bit of levity now and then."

"You're right. I doubt I'd be laughing if you weren't here."

"Well, I'm good for something then."

Chloe jabbed him in the ribs. "You're good for a lot. Stop fishing for compliments."

8

The train pulled into Munich Hauptbahnhof, the main train station, located in the centre of the city. The young English travellers gathered their belongings and began looking for a public telephone. Shep had studied possible accommodations, and they'd settled on the Bayerischer Hof, located in the city centre. It was classic and old, which they both adored.

When they arrived at the hotel, Shep turned to Chloe and asked, "All right, Pip. Shall I book one room for two, or two for one?" He knew the answer before he spoke, but it was fun to squabble with her.

"I think you know the answer to that question, Sheppard Sterling."

"I was just thinking of the cost," he grinned.

"Yes. So am I. I know very well what one room with two would cost me."

"Chloe. Don't you trust me?"

"No, Shep, I don't. Now go and book the rooms."

He went toward the front desk, chuckling to himself. After booking two adjacent rooms, they ascended to their floor in the lift. Chloe was enchanted with the accommodation. Although elegant, it was very inviting. They hadn't stayed anywhere so appealing since leaving England. They expected to have a longer stay in Munich. If things progressed as Chloe hoped, they would be visiting not one, but two people. She longed to find the answers she was seeking in Munich.

They unpacked their few belongings, meeting in Chloe's room half an hour later, to plan the next manoeuvre. They first searched the telephone directory, which was substantially larger than the one in Klasse. There were many Schoens, and an equal number of Wilts, both with varied spellings. Some had full names, and some only initials. After their discussion with Dieter, they weren't terribly anxious to face Wolfgang Wilt, so, Chloe and Shep concentrated upon Pieter Schoen. In spite of so many names, there was no Pieter listed. Not even a listing for Schoen with the initial P. That disappointed them greatly. Did it mean they would have to travel to another city? Could he be deceased? They turned to the Wilts, and began to run through the long list. Finally, they discovered a Wilt, followed by the initials 'W'' and 'R'. Dieter had said that Wolfgang's second name was Richard. Could it be him? Before impulsively dialling the telephone, they sat down in the chairs by the round table in the room and thought about what to do.

"This chap sounds rather unpleasant, Chloe. Are you sure you're prepared to meet him?"

"Oh Shep, I have to. If I don't, I'll always wonder. Especially since there is no Pieter Schoen listed in the directory. This Wolf creature may know what's become of Pieter."

"All right, but before we pay him a visit, let's go to the library and do some research. Dieter mentioned that Wolfgang's father's name was Karl and that he was very wealthy. Let's look at old microfilm records of newspaper articles. I'd like to know as much about Wolf as we can before meeting him."

"That's a good idea. I've no problem with doing that. I rather dread meeting him too. A little preparation won't hurt."

"Perhaps Dieter is remembering the young Wolf. People do mellow, you know. We might discover that he's a fine fellow after all."

"Don't be daft, Shep. Leopards don't change their spots that much."

"Yes, well, I'm afraid you're right there. So then, shall we have at it?"

They easily located the Bayerische Staatsbibliothek on Ludwigstrasse. The Ludwigstrasse was one of the city's four royal avenues. The city's grandest boulevard, with its public buildings, had maintained its architectural uniformity. It was designed, at the request of the king, as a grand street, worthy of the kingdom. Shep and Chloe couldn't help but see its beauty. Much of Munich had been completely destroyed during the war, but had also been totally reconstructed. It was a mixture of old and new, but during the restoration an excellent job had been done of keeping to the original grid and reproducing the lovely old buildings.

They entered the library, and climbed the beautiful staircase that immediately greeted visitors. Reading a directory, they were guided to an area that held a vast collection of newspapers and periodicals, all on microfilm. There were several rows of machines where the researcher could pop in a microfilm and scan its articles. They searched through the available years and requested 1939 to 1945. There was no way they would be able to complete all of them. Hopefully there would be listings of war casualties. They also meant to concentrate their attention on obituaries and business articles, keeping Wolfgang's father's name, Karl Wilt, in mind. Each sat down at a machine and began to read. It was very slow going. It was also hard not to get caught up in pictures and headlines about what was happening in the war during that time. Chloe's inability to read German hindered her progress. About all she could do was search out names. Shep, on the other hand, easily read through all articles of interest. Still, they found nothing of importance.

They took a break at lunchtime and visited a small café. Wondering if they should return for another session of grueling research, they almost came to the conclusion that enough was enough. But Chloe, with her somewhat stubborn streak, held firm. They *would* return. They decided that only Shep would read the microfilms, since Chloe wasn't really able to accomplish much. She sat beside him and scanned what he was reading. After an hour more, they both spotted a line that caused elation.

"Look, Chloe. Look. An article about the death of Karl Wilt. Egad! This is huge. Wait till you hear the details."

"What? When did he die? Please read it aloud."

"He died in 1944. He wasn't *that* old. Sixty-one years. Here's what it says;
Death of Karl Wilt

Karl Wilt, 61, well-known financier, businessman and philanthropist was found dead at his Grunewald home early on the morning of August 28, 1944. Herr Wilt was one of Germany's wealthiest philanthropists. Authorities were called to his palatial home shortly before 4:00 a.m. by his son, Wolfgang Wilt, who had just arrived home after serving several years in the military. Wilt told police that he had surprised his father, who apparently succumbed to a heart seizure upon seeing his son after such a long time. The son entered his father's bedroom while the elder Wilt slept, and gently woke him. The shock apparently caused his heart to stop. Karl Wilt was born in Klasse, Hesse-Darmstadt, on July 13, 1884. He graduated from the University of Heidelberg, and founded several successful companies during his lifetime. Herr Wilt fought valiantly for the Reichswehr from 1914 to 1918. He was married to Phyllis Schultz in 1919. One child, Herr Wolfgang Richard Wilt, was born of this union. Frau Phyllis Wilt died in 1940. Funeral arrangements are pending."

Chloe and Shep looked intensely at one another. "What an odd story," she murmured.

"Yes. Very odd. According to Dieter, Wolfgang was eagerly awaiting inheritance of his father's fortune. Surely he couldn't have done anything to help that along?" questioned Shep.

"I think that's entirely possible, but it would have been a bit difficult, wouldn't it? To stage a death to look like a heart seizure, when it was really murder?"

"Not really. I'm sure there are ways. It might be true that he caught him unawares, in his sleep. He probably planned to do so."

"Wouldn't there be any way the police could have detected that?" asked Chloe.

"It depends on how hard they were looking. That was a chaotic time. The war was still in progress. I imagine the police were very busy. There must have been chaos."

"I wonder what the mother died from. She was quite young."

"Yes. We don't know when she was born, but she could have been less than forty."

"It was during the war. Just at the beginning."

"Umm hmm. That's another titbit to look into," declared Shep. "So then. We now pay a visit to the 'not very pleasant' Wolfgang. Yes?"

"Yes. Gosh, Shep. I pray he isn't my father. I've never met him, but I know I'll despise him."

―――※―――

The two decided to wait until the following day before they continued their mission. Both were tired from their time at the library and looked forward to a good rest and a nice meal. They booked reservations in the hotel dining room for seven o'clock, and took leave of one another outside of their rooms.

Chloe bathed and changed into her one, formal gown. It had a white satin skirt and an amber-coloured cashmere top, with a rounded neckline and long sleeves. There was a matching coat in the same amber fabric, with three, large buttons on the front. She wore her hair in an upsweep. Short white gloves and amber high-heeled shoes completed the outfit. Chloe looked very chic and greatly resembled her mother at that age.

She met Shep in the hallway, and her heart did a little spin when she saw him. During their journey, he'd been mostly clad in corduroy trousers and jumpers, with white shirts underneath. Tonight he wore a very good-looking dark grey suit, and a white shirt with a striped tie. She asked herself why she'd never cared for him. In fact, she couldn't think of anyone she'd rather have been with than Shep. It was funny how a few years could make such a difference. They rode the lift to the restaurant and were shown to a nice, quiet table in the corner. Shep ordered a bottle of excellent wine. It was very nice to relax. There was no shortage of things to discuss, since they knew so much more than they had before leaving England.

"Shep, after meeting Dieter Schwab, I feel rather humbled. Here I am, fretting over my biological father's identity, when that poor soul has suffered such agony. My troubles seem so trivial compared to his."

Shep took a sip of wine and replied. "Yes, I know. If you compare the two situations, obviously, he's suffered massively. But Chloe, it doesn't mean that you're overreacting to what was done to your mother. The circumstances can't be compared. Dieter's awful injuries don't mean that the misery your mother endured isn't valid. Dieter's suffering is unspeakable. But, so was what happened to Elise. They're two separate kinds of suffering. You still have a right to know your father's identity. Only you can decide if your desire is strong enough for us to keep searching. I don't want you to believe there's something wrong with you because you feel the need to know who you are. Personally, I think it was probably healing for you to have discovered what Dieter went through. You've been so immersed in a need for justice. I've felt that way, too. After seeing him, there's no doubt that he's paid the full measure for his sins."

"Yes. You're right about that. Poor man. My heart aches for him. I understand what you're saying, but you have to admit that my problems seem trivial. They really can't be compared, can they? Seeing his condition puts things into perspective. Perhaps my mother wasn't wrong to just let God take care of the punishment."

"Chloe, you and your mother are different people. And remember, she isn't the one who abruptly found out that her father was a Nazi. You have a right to your reaction. Why? Are you telling me that you want to call a halt to this trip? Can you live without knowing the whole story?"

"I wish I could say yes. But I think it will eat at me all of my life. I don't know why it matters so much. I've had a wonderful life. What difference does it make?"

"I can't answer that. It's awfully complex, isn't it? You obviously have an innate need to avenge the evil that your mother endured. But, it's also deeper than that. I've never really known you well until these past few weeks. You appear to be quite a black and white person. You see things in absolutes. Things are either right or wrong, good or bad. Perhaps meeting Dieter broadened your thinking. Sometimes there's an in-between. The poor chap didn't have the maturity, or strength of purpose, to reject his companion's idea of an assault on your mother. It's hard to know what any of us would have done in similar circumstances. He made a terrible mistake. But he also learned from it, didn't he? Let's not forget that he was very young and he'd found himself in the midst of a war."

"Yes. My mother always taught me that everything in life happens for a reason. It would be easy to blame Dieter's misdeed for the horrors he endured later. But that seems too shallow. How many thousands of soldiers were horribly maimed, or didn't come home at all, and they never committed an atrocity like Dieter did?"

"Chloe, you're asking questions that there aren't any answers to. I'm a religious chap, to a degree. But to me, believing that all suffering is a direct result of some wicked act seems too simplistic. I know you've been taught that man has a free will. I certainly believe that. Supposedly the real justice comes later, after we're no longer here. Or, who knows? Maybe it all comes down to Karma. Or, maybe Christianity has the answer after all. He is terribly sorry for the wrong he did, and has asked for forgiveness. "

"Karma? The belief that if we don't live a moral life, we'll return as a cow?"

Shep laughed and drank some more wine. "No, Chloe. That's a Hindu view that many people from India believe. Actually the cow is sacred. No matter. I'm not going into my thoughts about Karma now. It would take the entire evening. Basically, it deals with our need to pay retribution for acts we committed in a prior life. But it's much deeper than that."

"My father believes he knew my mother in another lifetime – that they were soulmates. Do you believe in soulmates?"

"I don't disbelieve. In fact, I'll go one step further and say I think it's highly probable."

"Really? Shep, you surprise me."

"I take it you don't share my conviction."

"No. Well, I don't know. I don't know enough about the subject. I believe in Science. Hard, proven facts. The two don't complement one another. That's why I love medicine."

"Ah, but I believe they *do* complement one another. Science hasn't yet, definitively answered the really big questions about how we got here, and why. But, its science that will eventually answer them. I totally believe that. And, don't forget, not everything is hard fact. How do you explain animal instinct? There's no hard, fast fact there. I should think as an 'about to be veterinarian', you'd find instinct fascinating."

"I do, Shep. It's proof to me that God gave helpless animals a special gift – an inexplicable way to know what to do, and when to do it. Instinct often protects their lives. Human beings, too. No, that surely isn't something you can study under a microscope. To me, it certainly is proof of a higher power."

The waiter approached the table and the conversation stopped while they studied the menu and ordered. He poured them each another glass of wine.

"So then, how did we get off on this esoteric conversation?" Shep wondered aloud.

"Rambling from one subject to another. You asked if I felt vindicated after seeing Dieter and wanted to stop searching for more answers."

"And do you?"

"No. I'm dreadfully sorry for Dieter. But there were two other men involved in the attack. I don't think we're going to feel sorry for Wolfgang Wilt, and I have a horrible fear that he's my father."

"Then we need to continue. I suspect we're going to learn a lot more about the human mind before we go back to England, and I don't think it will all be black and white."

They enjoyed their marvellous dinner – the best since leaving England. After the dishes had been cleared away, Shep ordered a glass of Port and Chloe had a white crème de menthe. Then, they returned to their floor, feeling relaxed and content. Outside of Chloe's door, a serious look came over Shep's face.

"In case I've never told you before, Chloe Thornton, you're quite a remarkable girl. I'm awfully glad Violette suggested that I accompany you on this trip."

"Truthfully, Shep, so am I. I never thought I'd be saying this, but I've grown quite fond of you. You're very easy to be with, and I enjoy our conversations."

"So do I," he answered.

They were standing about two feet apart, looking intently into each other's eyes. Without even thinking, Shep leaned forward and placed his lips on hers. Chloe stepped toward him, and put her arms around his neck. She returned the kiss. It went on for quite some time, and when they stepped apart, both were breathing heavily.

"Too much alcohol," smiled Chloe.

"No. I've dined with many young ladies, and have had far more to drink than I did this evening. It isn't the alcohol, Chloe. Not for me. It's you."

"I know, Shep. I feel the same way. But, we can't let it go any further. Not now. We're here for a purpose. I don't want to be side-tracked with other emotions. Can't we wait, and sort out our emotional feelings after we've accomplished what we've set out to do?"

"Of course, Chloe. It makes me happy to think that you feel the same way I do. I'll let that be enough for now. I agree with you. We need to be able to put all of our energy into accomplishing our goals. So, scoot into your own room, before I change my mind," he laughed.

"I will. Good night, Shep. Thank you for a wonderful evening, and for being understanding. I'll see you in the morning."

Chloe turned and entered her bedroom. Shep sighed, straightened his shoulders, and continued to his own room, next door.

9

Shep and Chloe slept later the next morning. Each woke with more meaningful feelings for the other. Their short conversation had taken the relationship to a new level. Whatever the reason, there was an eagerness to be together and a sense of closeness when they greeted each other outside of their hotel rooms. Both sensed the change, but neither spoke of it.

They had breakfast in the restaurant on the rooftop, which afforded a splendid view of the city. It was a spectacular day, with blue skies and low humidity. Both of them had dressed nicely, since they were going to pay their long anticipated visit to Wolfgang Wilt. Chloe wore a white sleeveless, summer frock, simple and chic. Shep looked fresh and crisp in a white linen shirt, and beige trousers. His hair had grown longer since the last cut, some two weeks earlier, and Chloe liked it. Her own tresses fell into soft waves, touching her shoulders. They spread a map out on the table in front of them and studied the location of Herr Wilt's home. Apparently, he'd continued to live in the house that had been his father's. They recognised the name of the area from the obituary - Grünwald.

They had arranged the night before to hire a car and driver for the time they would be in Munich. They met the driver in the lobby of the hotel after breakfast. He spoke English well, and introduced himself as Michael

Landgarten. He told them that Grünwald was most definitely an up-scale area of Munich. It was located about twelve kilometres from the city centre and was well known because of an ancient castle located there. Grünwald was a domicile for many prominent people and was the wealthiest municipality in Germany. As their car rolled along, from the village of Harlaching onward, it was all wooded. After leaving the city they were surrounded by an abundance of green, and villas and gardens came into view. Luxury villas, generous detached houses, and high-class apartments in great gardens and parks marked the neighbourhood. It was apparently a sought-after place for the wealthy and prominent. Grünwald was full of traditional families with lots of property. Chloe and Shep were told that the nouveau riches made their homes in a different area near Starnberg.

They looked at each other and smiled. Since they both had grown-up in what would certainly be considered splendour, the size of the homes and the enormous pieces of land they sat on, weren't as impressive as they might have been to travellers from less affluent backgrounds. But, they were amazed at the overt display of wealth. There was glamour everywhere in the sophisticated neighbourhood. High gloss Porsche automobiles and Rolls Royce's turned out of broad gates; women strolled the streets in elegant apparel, swinging handbags that must have cost a fortune; babies were pushed in high, black prams by neatly dressed nannies. Needless to say, there was no poverty.

They hadn't telephoned ahead to make an appointment. After seeing where Wolfgang Wilt lived, they wondered if not having called was a big mistake. It seemed unlikely that doors were answered by the owners of such posh estates. Would they even be allowed to see Herr Wilt, if he had no idea they were coming? Whispering to one another about the dilemma, they asked Michael to find a telephone box where they might place a quick call. He did so, in rather short order. They debated whether Shep or Chloe should make the call and finally decided upon Chloe. After all, it was her mother who'd been attacked, and the man might be Chloe's biological father.

She climbed out of the car and entered the booth. Having written the number on a piece of paper back at the hotel room, she dialled and waited. Of course, the phone was picked up by a servant. Chloe asked if the woman spoke English and was pleased that the answer was yes. She then proceeded to inquire as to whether Herr Wolfgang Wilt was available. Again, to her satisfaction, the person at the other end asked her to wait a moment. The next voice she heard was a man's. Her legs began to tremble. Thankfully, he spoke English, as well.

"Herr Wilt, my name is Chloe Thornton. I apologise for calling on such short notice, but my companion and I have travelled from England, and we didn't know how to reach you until we arrived in Munich. Even then, we weren't certain you were the correct person. However, we're quite certain now. I need to speak with you in person, sir. My story is rather complicated and not easily told over the telephone. I assure you it is of grave importance, or I wouldn't have gone to all of this trouble to find you. Is there the slightest possibility that we might meet with you today? My friend and I are here, in Grünwald. We could come to your home any time you wish."

Chloe took a deep breath. She'd managed to say everything she wanted, before he'd had a chance to speak. She spoke rapidly, and it must have been clear to him that she was a bundle of nerves.

"You say your name is Chloe Thornton? I don't recall ever meeting anyone of that name."

"No, you wouldn't. It's my mother whom you've met. A long time ago, during the war, in France. Her name wasn't Thornton then."

"What was her name at that time?"

"Elise Lisak."

"I know no one of that name either. Lisak sounds like a peasant name."

Chloe was astounded. What a cheeky, rude man. But she'd already known that he wasn't a gentleman, so she held her tongue and ignored the barb.

"Herr Wilt, I wouldn't expect you to remember her name. That's why I need to speak with you directly. I promise that you *will* remember her when I remind you of the details."

"You have piqued my curiosity. Fortunately for you, I have no prior appointments today. So then, yes, I shall agree to see you and your friend. However, I bore easily, so don't expect to take too much of my time. I do hope this is worth my while. I'm an important man and don't like to waste time on trivial matters."

"I assure you this isn't a trivial matter. At least not to me."

"What is not trivial to you, may be of no interest to me whatsoever. Still, you may come to my home in an hour," he declared. It was said as though he were giving an order.

The phone line went dead and Chloe realised that he had hung up. She replaced the receiver and returned to the car. Shep was eagerly waiting to hear what had happened.

"Shep that was the cheekiest, nastiest man I've ever spoken with in my life. I hate the idea of meeting him. But we're here, and I'm not going to back out now.

She explained the conversation, word for word, and Shep looked appalled. Chloe was right. The man had no civilised manners.

"Well, it looks like we're in for a special treat, my little animal doctor," he chuckled. "Don't let his rudeness upset you. We were told to expect this. He's only reaffirming our suspicions."

"Shep. I just had an idea. I'd like to record what this ogre has to say. I don't even know if that's legal, but I want to be able to remember exactly what he says. Do you suppose he would have a tape-recorder?."

"Not a bad idea, Pip. A recording of this man might be worth some amusing moments later. Also, it would give your mother a chance to hear what he has to say. I'd think he would have a recorder. Judging from the size of the houses and the neighbourhood, he probably has everything imaginable. But, he'd have to let us use it, and agree to being recorded."

They asked Michael his opinion, since he was a German citizen. It turned out that he was quite well versed on the topic. He told them it was illegal to tape conversations in Germany without another's consent, and that there was no way it could be used in a court of law. However, he said that if they had the other party's consent, there was no problem. Shep asked him if *that* sort of tape could be used in a court of law, not that he had the slightest intention of using it against Wolfgang – unless he confessed to other, more recent rapes, or something of that sort. Michael's knowledge diminished at that point. He said he thought it could be used in some instances, perhaps in civil proceedings, but not criminal – or it might be the other way around. Shep didn't really care very much. They were only intending to tape the conversation if Wolf agreed. If they were going to use his tape recorder, he would know the reason why. As cheeky as he'd been on the telephone, he might just be arrogant enough to say yes.

Finally it was time to meet Herr Wilt. They returned to his villa, a sprawling residence, constructed of stucco. Michael let them out in the circular driveway and then parked his vehicle by the side of the house, inside of the wrought iron gates. Chloe and Shep approached the massive double front doors and rang the bell. A lovely Asian girl answered. She was dressed in the traditional garb of her native country– a silk robe, tied with an obi sash. She had long, silky, black hair and lovely features. The girl could easily have been doing more with her life than answering the door for a wealthy former Nazi. Perhaps she was his wife, but if so, she was awfully young. She certainly didn't look like one of Hitler's white, Aryan prototypes. In any case, she invited them inside and was very gracious. They were led to a big open living space, furnished with elegant items from the Orient. They both sat down on a long, low couch and waited to see what came next.

A few moments went by, and then a man entered the room. *He* could have passed for a member of Hitler's blonde-haired, blue-eyed, master race. Tall, nearly white haired, with a foreboding mouth and piercing blue eyes, Chloe and Shep knew immediately that it was Wolfgang Wilt. He looked evil. The temperature in the room seemed to drop, but it was probably Chloe's imagination. He walked slowly towards them and then stopped, looking them up and down. Finally, he spoke.

"So, you have come from England to speak with me. What an honour. Only a little over two decades ago, no one was coming from England to visit with Germans, unless they wished to drop bombs upon us."

Chloe ignored his statement. "Herr Wilt, my name is Chloe Thornton, as I told you on the telephone. This is my friend, Sheppard Sterling. It has taken a great deal of searching to find you. I am so anxious to know you better. May I ask if you might have a tape recording device? If so, I would greatly appreciate your permission to tape this conversation? As you know, I believe you knew my mother during the war. Since she is unable to be here with us, I'd like her to hear our discussion when I return home."

"I have no objection. Perhaps your tape will be worth money someday. I'm a wealthy, well-known man. Few people are fortunate enough to be allowed an intimate conversation with me."

He called for the maid and asked her to bring the recording device to them. She returned at once, placing it on the table. Shep looked it over, making certain there was tape in it. Then he switched it to the 'on' position.

"I'm perfectly aware of who you are," Herr Wilt continued. "You said I knew your mother. No, I never *knew* her. I knew her *body* quite well. She wasn't the sort I would have wanted to know in any other way. I got what I wanted from her and moved on with my life."

Chloe was livid and had to fight to keep from blurting out what she thought of him. But her motive in coming to meet this disgusting man was to learn more about him, and she wouldn't be able to accomplish that if she lost her temper. She sat silently, clasping her hands until the nails dug into her palms.

"Of course, you are the daughter of the French girl I had intimate relations with in 1940. I remember it well. You look like her. She was very good. Inexperienced, of course, but that is how I like them. She cried and struggled, which added to the excitement. I believe I had to slap her a time or two. She wouldn't calm down and submit. At first that's exhilarating, but it can become tedious after a time. She lived through it. I haven't thought of her since. What brings you to Germany?"

Chloe finally found her voice. It was shaky, but she managed to continue.

"I only recently learned about my mother's assault at your hands and those of your fellow soldiers. You see, she *didn't* get over it. She ended up with a child. *Me.* It was a devastating shock. One of the three of you is my father. I want to know who. I've already met Dieter Schwab and learned that it cannot have been him. He is incapable of conceiving children."

He burst into laughter. "So, old Dieter only shoots blanks? I should have known. I never liked him much. He wasn't the manly type. I'm surprised he's still alive."

"Yes, in a military convalescent home. He has no legs, and only one arm. It's pitiful."

"It is the result of war. If he'd been a better fighter, that wouldn't have happened to him. I have no pity for him."

"You sound as if you enjoy war," Shep said.

"War is the ultimate pleasure. Especially if one has the chance to kill another in a close and personal way. There is nothing more glorious than looking into the eyes of one who is about to die. The fear is overpowering. That's one of the things I enjoyed about your mother," he said, turning the conversation back to Elise. "She had tremendous fear in her eyes."

Chloe wanted to scratch *his* eyes out. She wasn't certain how much more she could take. He broached the subject of Chloe's paternity.

"So, you could be my daughter. I would not mind so much, except I do not like the brown eyes. They are a throwback, perhaps, to some defective ancestor. It is difficult to think that I could produce a child with brown eyes. As I recall, your mother had blue eyes. So, where do these brown eyes come from?"

"My grandfather was a handsome Russian. I inherited his warm, kind eyes."

"There are no handsome Russians, my dear girl. You obviously have little knowledge of the purity of races."

"I have enough to know that such a perverted mindset didn't spread across the globe. The Allies won the war, Herr Wilt."

"Ah, yes. The unfairness of it all. If the Americans had stayed on their side of the globe, we would easily have annihilated you Englanders. We nearly did. Then the so-called G.I.s -the mongrels - intervened."

"The war has been over for a long time now. Can we please move on to a more palatable subject?" Shep intervened.

Wolfgang Wilt turned and stared at him. "Why are you here, may I ask? Are you this little beauty's brother?"

"No. I'm a good friend. I also know her mother well. I didn't want Chloe to make this trip alone."

"Afraid I might to do her, what I did to her mother?"

"It's hard to believe that you could be so heinous as to refer to such barbaric behaviour, when Chloe could be your own flesh and blood."

"It would bring extreme pleasure. The idea of two bodies uniting in sexual union, when the same blood runs in the veins is very titillating."

"You are completely insane," Chloe cried.

"Do you think so, little one? Or perhaps you've only led a sheltered life. There are many pleasures in this world."

Chloe was trembling. She couldn't help it. The man was so utterly repulsive, and all she really wanted was to leave. But he was also fascinating. She couldn't believe for one moment that he was her father. Nor anyone's father, for that matter."

"Do you have children?" she managed to ask.

"I'm sure many exist, but they are unknown to me. They are probably wandering about Europe, homeless and poverty stricken, while their dear Papa lives in splendour. I like to think of that. I was the only child in my family. I never married. Thus, whatever offspring I have are illegitimate. Like you perhaps?"

"What of your mother and father?" Shep asked.

An odd look came over his face. "I have no mother and father. Not any longer."

"Were they killed in the war?"

"My mother was, in a manner of speaking."

"What does that mean?" Shep persisted.

"She was a Jewess. I didn't know that until the pogroms began. They were massive riots, aimed at the persecution and massacre of Jewish people. I took part in, and enjoyed them immensely. My mother, on the other hand, became very frightened. Finally, she confessed that her mother and father had been one hundred percent Jewish. I was appalled. It was intolerable. She had lied all of her life. That made me a full half Jew. It was enough for me to have been sent to a camp and exterminated. Me! There was no finer example of Hitler's dream. I wasn't having it. She had to go, before there could be any talk about my tainted heritage. "

"What do you mean, 'she had to go'?"

"I turned her in to the Gestapo. She was sent to Auschwitz, where she was part of the final solution. It was a great relief to have her gone."

"You turned your own mother in to the Gestapo? How could anyone do such a thing?" Shep asked, overcome with emotion.

"I simply told her that by going to a camp, she would be saving my life. She adored me and would never have wanted to place me in jeopardy. For a Jewess, she was a surprisingly courageous woman. She went without complaint. I'd like to have seen her go to the gas chamber. I imagine she showed the same remarkable bravery. But, what's done is done."

"How could your father have allowed such a thing?"

"He never knew that I was involved He had known from the time he married her that she was Jewish. He had lied to me, too. I had a friend in the *Hitler Youth* turn my mother in to the authorities. Otherwise, they might have come after me, too. I made certain to be away, and they didn't even know of my existence."

Neither Chloe nor Shep could speak. How did one respond to such evil? Wolfgang clapped his hands together.

"So, how then can I help you? You want to know whether I am your father. There is no way to tell, is there? I suppose we could compare blood types. I know mine. It is Type O. What is yours?"

Chloe gulped. "I'm type O, too. So is my mother."

"This does not make it definitive, you know. Obviously, you could be my daughter. But we would need to know Pieter Schoen's blood type as well. It may well be O, too. The only thing it proves is that nothing is ruled out. I should imagine you would like very much to find that you carry my genes. I am a wealthy man and one to be emulated. I would have to do a lot of thinking, since your brown eyes are a bother to me, but it isn't inconceivable that I would allow you to move to Germany and live with me. After enough years, I might be satisfied that you would be suited to be my heiress. A nice windfall for you, no? Perhaps you inherited my mother's eyes. That would be abhorrent. I certainly do not want any little Jewish offspring. That line is dead and gone. It travels through the mother, you know."

"Herr Wilt, I am the adopted daughter of a member of the aristocracy in England. My father is an earl. We live in a mansion that puts your humble abode to shame. Your money means absolutely nothing to me. I would never consider spending one day of my life with someone like you. Frankly, I think you belong in a mental facility."

Shep was surprised at Chloe's outburst. But, he certainly couldn't blame her. The man was odious. It was obvious that Chloe no longer cared whether she could learn more from him. Shep was only apprehensive because Wolfgang seemed so totally immoral and clearly capable of any sort of cruelty. He broke into the conversation before Wolfgang had a chance to speak.

"Herr Wilt, probably the most helpful thing you could do would be to give us any information you might have about Pieter Schoen. Now that we've met both you and Dieter, the only one left would be Pieter. Once we speak to him, we can leave Germany and go home."

"May I ask why? Since my probable daughter has such disdain for me, why is she interested in learning the truth about her biological father?"

"Because, even if I'm disgusted with my findings, I have a need to know who I am. That isn't unusual among adopted children."

"Apparently the identity of your father holds more interest for you than it does for me. It is, I admit, an interesting concept. The idea that two people can physically connect and form another being is thought provoking. But as far as emotion, or some sort of attachment, it is so much foolishness. I could no more love you than your adopted father does."

"I beg your pardon. My adopted father loves me a great deal. Blood connection isn't the be-all and end-all. Look what you did to your own mother. The woman who gave you life. How abhorrent."

"Well then, I expect you'd be even more repulsed if you knew what happened to my father."

"There is probably very little you could tell me that would be surprising." Chloe replied. "It's clear you're capable of anything. Not only that, you seem proud of the evil things you've done." She glanced at the recorder, as the tape wound slowly round, capturing each word that was spoken.

"Indeed, I *am* proud. Not many men would have the emotional strength to carry through with their fantasies."

"Such as . . . ." questioned Chloe.

"Would you like to hear about what happened the night I returned from the war?"

"Not particularly, but I suspect we're going to anyway. It's been clear to me for quite some time that you have a strong need for self-aggrandisement. So, go ahead."

"Ah, you mock me. When I tell this story, remember, if I could do such a thing to my own father, imagine what I'd be capable of doing to you, or your milquetoast friend," he said, pointing to Shep.

Both Chloe and Shep smirked. They'd begun to realise that the egocentric psychopath who stood in front of them was more likely to brag about his depraved deeds if goaded by disinterest and an attitude of absurdity. They glanced at one another and grinned, as if to say 'What a dolt.' It had the desired effect.

"On the night I returned from the war, my father wasn't expecting me. I wasn't mustered out in the usual way. Actually, I was dishonourably discharged, which brought me great joy, since I had grown very bored with the whole mess. In the beginning, I enjoyed the killing immensely. But after a while, it all became routine. The enemy wasn't even surprised anymore when a gun was pointed at their heads. They'd become what everyone called 'battle hardened'. It was just the same thing over and over again. I broke the boredom by keeping a full canteen of Schnapps at all times. I knew I'd be able to return to my father's home and resume my life in and around Grünwald. One of my greatest pleasures had been to kill the woodland creatures who roam all over this property. Now *there* is a way to see fear in its most primitive state. A pregnant doe, grazing placidly in a meadow, looks at the person who is about to take her down with raw panic in her eyes. She knows what is about to happen, and there is nothing she can do. But, I go astray."

Chloe felt that she might be ill. She wondered if it were all a ruse to make them think he was a vicious brute. Could such a person actually exist?

10

"So, I shall continue, yes?" He nodded his head at Chloe and Shep, who still sat on the uncomfortable sofa.

Chloe spoke up. "Sir, if you don't mind, I need to use your facilities. I'm interested in what you have to say, but I won't be comfortable and able to listen intently unless I can go to the toilet."

"Yes, of course. Perhaps we should all take a short break. There is so much to tell, isn't there?"

"Where would I find the facilities?"

"There are many, of course. The nearest is on this floor, down the hallway to the right, and then on the left. Another can be found down that hall," he pointed behind them, "straight at the end. You're welcome to use either of them. While you're availing yourself of my hospitality, I'm going to tell Fang Lu to prepare some aperitifs and snacks. You must be growing hungry."

Chloe smiled to herself. She couldn't imagine how the disgusting man could possibly think anyone would have an appetite in his presence. In fact, it was just the opposite. She was extremely nauseous and needed to leave his presence for at least a few minutes. Perhaps a drink of water would help. She chose to use the washroom straight down the hallway from where they were sitting. She briskly walked toward it, over the polished teakwood floors.

Wolfgang disappeared in the other direction, purportedly toward the kitchen area. Chloe was glad for a respite. Listening to such a monster was difficult. Especially when he made references to her own mother. The thought of his ever having laid a hand on Elise was chilling. Chloe had new respect for her mother's strength. She was certain that if she'd gone through the same ordeal, she would never have escaped with her mind intact.

After reaching the toilet, Chloe emptied the contents of her stomach. She's been afraid that would happen. The comment about the pregnant doe had done it. She wiped a cold cloth over her forehead, and waited a moment until she felt a bit better. Glancing into the mirror, Chloe could see the effect his words already had upon her. She looked pale and wan, and there was fear in her brown eyes. Brown eyes, she thought. The monster's eyes were a piercing blue. Elise's were a lovely shade of cerulean blue. She glanced upwards and closed her eyes. *Please let these eyes be a sign that I am in no way related to this monster*, she silently prayed. Upon her return to the living area, Wolfgang was more than ready to launch into the story about his father's death. His eyes were sparkling with the memory. The tale began.

"My father didn't know I was returning. I pondered what to do about him all of the way home. I knew he'd put up a terrible fuss when he heard I'd been discharged. I had no intention of putting up with him. On top of that, I had no intention of having to spend my life living under the same roof with him, or worse, having to find employment. He believed that offspring should work. So, upon my arrival, I crept into the house in the middle of the night. Knowing he would be asleep, I quietly made my way to his room. He was lying on his back, snoring like a bear. I'd brought a pillow from the spare room. It was one of the easiest things I've ever done. Child's play, really. I simply placed the pillow over his head and held it there. Of course, I'd caught him off guard. He struggled a bit, grunting, groaning, and making disgusting noises, but finally that stopped. I continued to hold the pillow in place until I was certain he was gone. When I removed it, he didn't even look like he'd been through anything dreadful. He just looked like he'd fallen asleep and never woke."

"But he was your own father. Did you hate him so?" asked Shep.

"No, not at all. He wasn't a bad sort. We'd had our good times. But he wouldn't have fit in with my plans for the future. It was time for him to join my mother."

"What did you do with his body?" asked Chloe.

"That wasn't my responsibility. I rang the local authorities, and they came. I told them that he had awakened when I arrived, and had appeared to suffer a heart seizure. It was determined that was what had happened, due to the excitement of seeing me after such a long time. Remember, it was during the war. There were a lot more things to worry about than a death in bed of a wealthy man in Grünwald. No one would ever have thought that I had anything to do with it. I'm very good at acting as though I have emotions when necessary."

"Have you no conscience?" asked Shep.

"I don't suppose so. Not as you'd define it. I don't believe in good, bad, or evil. We have to do things in life to further our own goals. Sometimes those things aren't pleasant, but they have to be done."

Both Chloe and Shep couldn't wait to get out of the man's house. He made their skin crawl. It appeared that the time to end their wretched visit with Wolfgang had finally arrived. They thanked him graciously, if insincerely. Chloe had only one more thing she wanted to know.

"Herr Wilt, earlier we spoke of Pieter Schoen. Then, I believe we got sidetracked and never returned to the subject. I'm awfully curious to speak with him, too. If I'm able to do so, and can determine what blood type he has, it would help toward solving my problem. I would think you'd like to know the truth, too. Have you any idea where I might find him? Dieter thought he might be here in Munich."

"Yes. I believe he is. He's turned out to be the worst disappointment of all."

"How do you mean?" asked Chloe.

"He's a Christian. A radical Christian. Not just a member of a Christian church, but a *part* of a religious order. He's a monk. Can you imagine? Why anyone would choose such an occupation is unbelievable. I wouldn't speak to him if I passed him on the street."

Chloe couldn't help but laugh to herself. This horrible man, who had admitted to murdering his own father, and sending his mother to the gas chamber at Auschwitz, wouldn't speak to an old military friend who was now a monk. *Please, please God,* she silently prayed. *Do not let this man be my father.*

It was time to leave. Chloe reached out and shook his hand. "Thank you again for listening to my tale. It was interesting to meet you."

While Chloe was saying her goodbyes, Shep extracted the tape from the recording machine and slipped it into his trouser pocket.

"When shall I meet you again, Fraulien?" Wolf asked.

Never, thought Chloe.

However, aloud she told him that she would speak to him after she'd found Pieter Schoen. Wolfgang added, at the last moment, that he thought he knew the monastery where Pieter was domiciled. Its' name was St. Francis of Assisi Abbey. It was a Benedictine monastery located in Maxvorstadt, Munich. Chloe was delighted to have the information. Obviously Wolfgang had known it all along, but had only decided to share the information when he thought it might somehow induce her to return and see him again.

Wolfgang took both of her hands in his. "I suspect we are father and daughter. I have uncanny senses about such things. Since I have no relations, I should like knowing there is someone to whom I might leave my fortune. If we could only do something about the brown eyes – perhaps these new contact lenses one hears about."

"That's a possibility, Herr Wilt," Chloe responded. She just wanted to leave. Pulling her hands back, she said goodbye once again. Together, Chloe and Shep hurried outside and tried to walk normally to the car. Wolfgang stood in the open doorway, looking like a jolly German host, waving his guests off. The moment they were far enough from the house so that they couldn't be overheard, Shep turned on Chloe.

"What the bloody hell was that all about? How could you treat him at all decently? You're just as daft as he is. Maybe you *are* his daughter."

Chloe turned on him with blazing eyes. "That isn't funny, Shep. Not one bit funny. I *had* to be civil to him, to get the information I wanted. He's a madman. A grotesque, psychotic, madman. God help me, if he *is* my father."

"Shep quickly changed his tune. I was joking. There's no way. I thought you'd pass out when he talked about shooting the deer, not to mention other woodland creatures. It's good you didn't tell him your career plans. He probably would have suggested a little hunting foray."

Chloe shuddered. "We can discuss this later, Shep. Right now, I want to take the tape to the police. Surely they're not going to ignore his confessions."

"Chloe, how do we prove that Wolfgang gave his consent for us to tape him?"

"It's on the recorder. When Fang Lu set it on the table, I only adjusted the volume. It was already running. Everything he said, including giving his consent, is on there."

"My god, Pip. You should have been a detective."

"Being in the medical profession isn't so far off, really."

"No. I suppose you're right. So, we go to the police. Then what?"

"Then our concern about Wolfgang is over. We try to find Pieter Schoen. He can't be any worse than Herr Wilt."

Once in the car, Michael listened to their instructions about going to the police, and he turned the car in the appropriate direction. There was a police station within a few miles, and Chloe was relieved to see it. She wanted to be rid of the tape, as well as any thoughts of the disgusting Wolfgang Wilt. They entered the station and were met by another model of German pride. Blonde and blue-eyed, with a mouthful of perfect white teeth, he would have been Hitler's dream. *My god*, thought Shep. *Are there no other types of people in this country?* Then he pulled up short, realizing that through the genocidal actions of a madman, there was a lot of truth to his previous thought. It made his blood run cold.

The policeman was very cordial. He spoke excellent English and asked how he could be of assistance. They presented a short version of their experience. After listening to them, he invited Shep and Chloe to join him in a room to the rear of the building. Several other officers joined them. Chloe explained, at length, the reason they had been in Herr Wilt's home. In the course of the conversation, the tape recording of the entire visit was produced. There, sitting on a tabletop, was a record of Wolfgang Wilt calmly and clearly admitting to the murder of his father, the rape of a young girl in France in 1940, deportation of his own mother to the gas chambers at Auschwitz, and various other depraved acts.

11

Chloe and Shep were certain that the tape would be stunning to the authorities. It *had* to contain enough information to arrest Wolfgang on murder charges. Chloe was enormously relieved. They had stumbled into the morass with no forewarning. At that point, all she really wanted was to go back to England. When the tape had been played through twice, everyone at the table sat back. Chloe and Shep waited for one of the officers to congratulate them on a job well done. Instead, they all burst into laughter.

"What the devil is going on here?" asked Shep, annoyed. "We've just brought you evidence that this man is guilty of numerous ghastly crimes, and you're laughing."

One of the older officers spoke up. "We apologise, Herr Sterling. It's just that this is not anything new. It's only Wolfgang, playing his usual role. That of the mad, evil, criminal. Let me explain. To begin with, Wolfgang's father's death was thoroughly investigated at the time. He was not smothered to death. He died of an aortic aneurysm. He had been dead for hours before his son found him. We traced back to the time Wolfgang arrived in Munich, and when he was left by a taxicab at his father's residence. He had nothing to do with his father's death. It *is* highly probable that he *did* turn his mother in to the Gestapo. The police even had him examined by more than one, very well-known psychiatrist. He certainly suffers from mental problems, but they stem from the guilt he carries over the few really evil things he *has* done in his life. What he did to his mother is probably one of those; what he did to *your* mother is undoubtedly another. If we could have, we would have prosecuted on that act, but the statute of limitations has run out. All of his talk about how much he enjoys killing is so much foolishness. He was drummed out of the military because he refused to fight. He was branded a coward. Actually, while a pathetic quitter, he does do good things for others. He heads up a foundation that provides care and hope to homeless children, who are victims of the war. He has received several awards for his work with such orphans. So, you see, you have been duped. You're not he first. He does this frequently."

Chloe and Shep were astounded. They tried to argue, pointing out various places on the tape where he had sounded so chillingly believable. But the police had been through it all before. Many times, apparently. He was never far from their radar. The good citizens of Munich, and especially Grünwald, were aware of his peculiarities. But, the good he did for others made up for the lies he told.

"It isn't surprising that he seemed somewhat taken with you. The truth is, he undoubtedly would give an arm and a leg to have a daughter. While I can't say with certainty, my guess is that he is completely incapable of reproduction. There is no question that he has a nasty record when it comes to sexual issues. He has always been known to frequent the red light district. When he was examined by physicians, it was noted that he has been infected many times by a wide variety of venereal diseases. This is by his own admission, although one has to take into account his propensity for lying. Still, physicians have stated that they believe past disease has rendered him sterile. Whether that would go back to 1940, I have no idea," said the senior officer, who seemed to have an enormous amount of information about Herr Wilt.

Chloe smiled for the first time. "I would love to think you're right about that. It wouldn't be pleasant to think that he had a venereal disease when he raped my mother."

"Whether he is, or isn't your father, Fraulein, you are clearly nothing like him. One can see that you are decent, and pardon the expression, but well bred. You must, indeed, take after your mother."

"Yes, many people say that," Chloe answered.

"So, we do thank you for your concern and for bringing your conversation with Herr Wilt to our attention. But allow your minds to rest. He is what an American friend of mine would call a 'bag of wind.'"

Chloe and Shep laughed. The description did fit Wolfgang to a tee.

"So," said Shep. "It's time we were on our way. We have one last stop to make in Munich, and then we'll return to England. We appreciate your help."

"We're glad you came to us. Don't hesitate to contact us again while you are here in Munich. We are here to assist in any way. May I ask where you are staying?"

"Yes, certainly. We're at the Bayerischer Hof."

"Lovely place. Don't judge all of Germany by your experiences with Herr Wilt. The past is behind us. Germany is as glad of that, as you in England are. The war was a time of madness. Try to see the good in our city and our country."

"Yes, we have. We've grown to like Germany a lot. Thank you for your honesty, and for taking so much time with us. Actually, it's a great relief to know that what we heard was rubbish."

Chloe and Shep left the station, returned to their waiting car and the ever patient Michael.

"Where to now?" he asked.

"Back to the hotel first, for a bite to eat and a lie-down. Then, what do you think, Chloe?"

"I hate leaving Germany without speaking to Pieter. After having spent time with Wolfgang, nothing can be any shoddier. I feel as though I'm in worse shape now than I was when I started this quest. The idea of returning to England, with even the remote possibility that Wolfgang Wilt could be my biological father, is enough to make me ill."

"Don't you feel somewhat better after speaking to the police? I know I do."

"Yes. I suppose. But he still makes me feel crawly all over."

"Well, we know where Pieter is, if Wolfgang was telling the truth. It shouldn't be hard to find him. I agree with you that it would be a mistake to leave without meeting him. Then, we'll at least have accomplished what we set out to do. We'll have found and talked to all three of the men who assaulted your mother."

They returned to their rooms and took a two hour break to order room service and rest for a spell. Michael was instructed to pick them up outside of the hotel, in their usual spot, at two o'clock. Chloe wondered if she should ring Pieter. Shep said he doubted that a monastery had telephones. So they decided to take their chances. Anyway, it seemed like they'd had quite good luck when they'd showed up unannounced to meet the other men from Elise's past.

In the meantime, Shep wondered about ringing Violette. He hadn't spoken with her in several days and thought he should bring her up-to-date. He finally put a call through, and was glad to find her available. They had a short conversation during which he told her where they were and a little bit about what had happened. It would have taken an hour to explain everything. He said they planned on seeing the last of the three men, and then hoped to return to England. He thought they would be on an aeroplane in two days.

Violette was happy to hear that the trip was nearly over. In her opinion, little had been accomplished, but if Chloe was more settled in her mind, then perhaps it had been worth it. The important thing was that nothing bad had happened to either of the young people. Shep did explain that they'd had a long conversation with the police, that had yielded a significant amount of information about one of the men involved in the rape of Elise. Apparently he was well known to them. Shep said that he would go into all of the details when he was back at *Coeur Jolie*.

After hanging up, he relaxed and tried to prepare himself for the final confrontation. He would be glad to leave Germany and return to his homeland. But he would miss seeing Chloe every day. It had been a gigantic awakening to find that he was very attracted to her. He wondered if she had the same feelings. From what she had said the night they had dined at the hotel, it was certainly plausible. The truth was, he had always been attracted to her. Who wouldn't have been? She was a very engaging sort of girl. On their first meeting, they'd both been so young and naïve. Neither had ever been involved with someone of the opposite sex. Shep had developed into a very handsome chap, but he still saw himself as someone whom the likes of Chloe Thornton would never find appealing. He was somewhat frightened to make his feelings known. It always seemed easier to laugh and joke with her. Still- he had been honest that one, special night, and she had reciprocated. He had hopes for the future.

At a quarter to two, Shep tapped on her door, and she immediately opened it. As always, she looked adorable. She wore a pink, A-line, pique dress, with cap sleeves and a jewel neckline. It was a simple outfit, yet Chloe always managed to turn anything she wore into a fashion statement. Her lovely hair was arranged in a low chignon, and she wore minimal cosmetics. Shep was always so proud to be seen with her. He had no way of knowing that Chloe had the same feelings about him. Just as he was reluctant to show his growing feelings toward her, she was also apprehensive. She knew Shep liked her, but it was a giant leap from friendship to more profound feelings. The whole concept of love was new to her. She had immersed herself in her studies all of her adult life, never giving any thought to matters of the heart. She'd always assumed that things like love and marriage would take care of themselves in time. Now, she wondered if that time had arrived.

The two descended to the lobby and out of the front doors to the car. They greeted Michael and, once settled, drove in the direction of The Abbey of St. Francis of Assisi in Maxvorstadt. Michael explained that the area where the Abbey was located was very difficult for automobiles to negotiate. There was apparently limited parking available for outsiders. He suggested that they leave the car at Marienplatz, the city centre, and walk from there. According to him, it would be a short trip, just a few streets north. Because Michael was the expert, no one argued, and soon they were on foot. Maxvorstadt had some interesting sights, not least of which was an address where Adolf Hitler had once lived, as well as numerous fine art museums. It was heavily populated by students.

Finally, they reached the abbey. It was relatively new, having been destroyed during the war and only partially rebuilt since. They entered by the main door, where a large bell hung on a pull. Michael reached up and yanked it. Almost immediately, an elderly gentleman in white robes appeared. He was most courteous, and once again, spoke perfect English.

"How may I help you?" he asked, bowing slightly.

"We were hoping to be able to visit one of your residents. His name is Pieter Schoen. At least that was his name. I apologise for being so ignorant, but do monks take new names?" asked Shep.

"He is called Brother Pieter. He seldom has visitors. I am sure he will be delighted that you have come. Follow me please. I will take you to him."

They proceeded down a long, cool hallway with stone floors and stucco walls. Everything was spotlessly clean, and it was exceedingly quiet. No one spoke as they walked along. At last they came to a rounded doorway, near the end of the corridor. Their host rapped on the wood. There was a short wait, and then it was opened. A nearly bald, middle-aged man stood in the doorway, dressed in the same white robe. He had a ruddy face and a warm smile. He seemed kind. Chloe was impressed with his appearance, and for a moment she was thrown awry, almost forgetting the purpose for their visit.

Brother Pieter tilted his head to one side, questionably. "You wish to see me?" he asked.

"Yes…yes," she stuttered. "Brother Pieter. My name is Chloe Thornton, and this is my friend, Sheppard Sterling. We've come from England to see you. Actually, your old military friend, Wolfgang Wilt, told us where we could find you."

"Wolfgang? I haven't seen him for many years. Since before the war ended." He scowled. "Why don't we go to the visitor's lounge? I'm afraid you would find my living quarters a bit cramped for a conversation. I assume you are here for a conversation?"

"Yes, we are. Wherever you think would be appropriate is fine," Chloe answered.

They walked back down the stone corridor, stopping beside a door which led to a large room with a fireplace and comfortable looking armchairs. The floor was stone, but there was a rug covering it. He stood back, motioning them to enter. After Shep and Chloe were inside, everyone sat down.

"Now, I'm curious," Brother Pieter smiled. "Why would two young people come all the way from England to Germany to pay a visit to an old, uninteresting man, who lives a secluded life in a monastery?"

"We think you may have lived a rather more interesting life before you came here," Shep answered. He didn't smile.

Pieter looked at him solemnly. "I have had a varied life, Mr. Sterling. As to whether it has been interesting, I leave that for others to decide."

"Yes, well, the point is Brother Pieter, I think you may have known my mother, Elise Lisak, back in France. You met her the day that evacuations from Dunkirk were taking place. It was in a small farmhouse, near Bergues?"

Brother Pieter looked blank for a moment, and then his face flushed. "So, I have not left the past behind after all. I had rather hoped to have done so."

"Then you know to what I'm referring?" Chloe asked.

"I believe I do. Can you explain a bit further?"

"You were with your two friends – Dieter Schwab and Wolfgang Wilt. You burst into my mother's farmhouse and assaulted her. She was young and very innocent. Does that help your memory?"

"Regrettably, yes. I was there. I have spent the rest of my life wishing I could undo the events of that day."

"So has my mother, I'm afraid. For that matter, so have I. You see, I am a constant reminder of what happened that day, because I am a product of the assault."

"Do you mean that you were conceived that day? Your mother conceived a baby when we – when we – visited her?"

"Yes, when you raped her."

Brother Pieter placed his hands together, as if in prayer, and lowered his head. Apparently, he *was* praying. He said nothing for quite a spell. Finally, he raised his head and looked Chloe straight in the eye.

"I am so sorry. So terribly sorry. It was an evil act. I knew it then, and I should never have been a part of it."

"Yet you were."

"Yes. I don't deny that. Have you only now learned about your paternity? Is that why you've come, after so many years?"

"Yes. I overheard a conversation between my mother and a friend. It was a tremendous shock. I don't think I've recovered from it yet. I'm hurt and angry that my mother endured such violence. Furthermore, I'm infuriated that you and the others weren't punished. And of course, I'd like to know the identity of the man who fathered me."

"I'll be happy to answer any questions that I can. Would you like an explanation for my behaviour that day?"

"I can't imagine there could be any sane explanation. But yes, I'd like to try to understand why someone would participate in such heinous activity."

"Oh, my dear young lady. How many times have you heard the expression 'the flesh is weak'? I was a foolish, stupid, young man. A follower, not a leader. Wolfgang was the leader. But it makes no difference. I knew right from wrong. I didn't listen to God's voice inside of me, saying that it would be a grave sin. I could never have done such a thing on my own. But, young men can be such fools when they become immersed in a sort of 'pack' mentality. What can I say? There is no excuse. I have truly lived with the guilt of that act all of my life. Now, here you are to tell me that another life was created that day. As to whether I am the one responsible for that, how can I know? I have never married. Never had children. That is what a profound influence it had upon me. You are a lovely, perfect example of God's work. I would be happy to be able to say that you are my child. But I simply have no idea."

"What is your blood type?" Shep asked.

"I am type O. I remember from the war."

"Yes, well, so am I," replied Chloe. "However, it appears that everyone associated with this sordid mess is type O. Wolfgang, my mother, me, and now you. I don't know about Dieter, but it doesn't matter. He's unable to have children and always has been."

"So that means it is either Wolfgang or me."

"Sir, I cannot help but notice that you have brown eyes, like Chloe," Shep interrupted.

Chloe had noticed them too, when she first saw Brother Pieter. They'd sent a shiver down her spine.

"Yes. I see that too. My mother had brown eyes. None of the others did. If I recall, your own mother has lovely blue eyes," Pieter responded.

"She does. But my grandfather was Russian. I've always believed that my eye colour comes from him."

"Certainly, that is likely. If I remember my studies in biology, from long ago, if one parent has brown and one blue, then the brown would be dominant. I don't recall much more than that. I don't know how the grandparent would fit into the equation."

"It's quite complex. There's no way to know for certain where my brown eyes originated. Yours are brown, and we know that one of two men is responsible for my conception. That would lend credence to the suspicion that you're my biological father. If it's between you or Wolfgang, I suspect it's you."

"Pardon me, if I am too outspoken, but does it matter? I assume from your surname that you were either adopted or are married."

"I was adopted when my mother married Sloan Thornton in 1946."

"Then, to my way of thinking, *he* is your father. Didn't he raise you to become the fine young lady you appear to be? Did he treat you well, and perform all of the duties one would expect from a father?"

"Yes, he did. He was the most wonderful father a girl could have. But you see, I'm afraid he may only have done those things because he loved my mother and wanted to please her."

"While I don't know this Sloan Thornton, I suspect you are wrong. It would be a hard role to play for years on end. Love is not easy to pretend, don't you think?"

"I don't know."

"I suspect you do, but it isn't for me to argue. I don't say these things in an attempt to lessen the blame on myself. As I said before. It would make me very proud to think I had helped to create the charming, young lady I see in front of me. But I would never say that I am her father. I did nothing to earn the right to that title. Sloan Thornton did the difficult part."

Chloe had tears in her eyes. "I simply want all of this to go away. I wish I could return to my safe world – the world I knew before overhearing the truth."

"Truth is a difficult concept. There are many truths in life, dear Chloe. If truth is reality, then your reality seems to be that you clearly have only one father, Sloan Thornton. Can you tell me why it matters so much which of we three scoundrels planted the seed?"

"I don't know. I'm not sure it does matter so much anymore. I thought it did. I thought I needed to know who I am. Without knowing who planted the seed, as you put it, I don't feel I'll ever really know who I am."

"And who are you, Chloe Thornton? What are your beliefs and values; your hopes and dreams?"

"I'm a very mixed-up young lady," she laughed ruefully. "But before this happened I was a bright, happy person, who knew exactly where her life was going. I've just completed a study of veterinary medicine. I sat for my exams before I left England and soon will be a registered animal physician. I don't need to add that I adore animals. I've always wanted to devote my life to working with them. You ask what my values and beliefs are. I believe in good triumphing over evil; I believe in kindness and compassion; I believe people should help one another. Perhaps I'm too simplistic. I think I would have killed you, if I'd been my mother. Although I'm very moral, I don't think it would have been wrong for her to have killed all of you."

"No. If she could have accomplished such a feat, it would probably not have been wrong. It would have been self-defence. But you see, I don't believe she could have accomplished that. There were three of us and only her – a slender young girl. Who knows how much worse we might have hurt her? We were beneath human."

"I still wish she had tried. I even wonder if she would have been better off to have died trying."

"So, you're angry with your mother for not behaving as you think you would have?"

"Perhaps," Chloe murmured.

"Perhaps she also believed that good triumphs over evil. There was no need for her to try to kill us, only to have died in the process. If she believed that God would take care of the evil, it wasn't up to her to mete out the punishment."

"You're very wise, aren't you?"

"Not so very. Just older, and able to view things from a different perspective. I have to say I think God *has* dealt with the evil. Who has a happier life today, Chloe? You've now met all three of us. Are any of us happier than your mother?"

"No. My mother has a wonderful life."

"And, what about you? Are we happier than you? Will the legacy we leave be better than yours?"

"I can't imagine that it will be. I hope that I'll live a good life and accomplish important things."

"Need I say more?"

Chloe looked at the floor, tears still welling in her eyes. Brother Pieter made sense. His last questions had great impact. Why hadn't she thought of them? Everything seemed so clear. Suddenly, she wanted very much to go home. She wanted to hug her mother, and tell her father that she loved him. But, by the same token, she wasn't sorry she'd made the journey. In time she would have reached the same conclusions on her own, but looking at it through the eyes of one of the perpetrators had strongly influenced her thinking.

"Your pain touches my heart, and I wish I could wipe it away. It isn't a good feeling for one to know that he caused such grief in another person. Your mother must have suffered dreadfully, too. I wonder if she would ever have found the happiness she now enjoys, if she hadn't experienced such terror. So often, that's the way life works. We can't fully experience joy, unless we first know despair. But, that is my belief. Perhaps you don't see the truth in such reasoning. Yes, I wish I could erase your pain. But only you, with God's help, can do that. God helped me to understand that the only way I could come to grips with my conscience – with the evil that I'd done to your mother – was to relinquish my own happiness; to spend my life in prayer, doing penance, in an attempt to cleanse my own soul. Perhaps that seems simplistic to you. Perhaps you will think that I only hid away from the world, refusing to allow temptation to overtake me again. But living as a monk is not an easy path. There are temptations in my world, too. Mostly, however, I've missed the joy of living a *whole* life. I wasn't cut out for the religious life. It wasn't what I might have chosen. But, there was no question that I had to pay. At least that was, and still is, my belief. I think every one of us – Dieter, Wolfgang and me – has paid in his own way."

"What would you have done if the nightmare in the farmhouse had never taken place?" Chloe asked.

"Oh my, so many different things. I would have married. I have missed the warmth of another human being. I would have used the gift of a good mind to study, and probably to teach. Choosing St. Francis as my patron Saint wasn't an accident. I too, love animals. I would have lived in the country, surrounded by beautiful, living creatures; caring for them, and loving them. I purposely chose a monastery in an urban environment, because it forced me to give up the dream of a pastoral existence. But, don't feel sorrow. There can be great happiness in knowing God. Nevertheless, I fight against the appeal of the secular world a thousand times a day."

"Do you never think of leaving this life? Haven't you paid the penalty? You could still realise many of your dreams. It isn't too late," Chloe answered.

"No. I wouldn't trust myself to do so. If I harboured the capability to commit such a vile, sinful act when I came upon your mother, perhaps that possibility still exists. I'm still a man, Chloe Thornton. Not a saint."

Chloe impulsively reached for Brother Pieter and hugged him.

"Thank you, Brother Pieter. Thank you for using your gift of wisdom to help me sort through what I'm feeling. You've truly made me look at this dilemma in a different light. I won't forget you. I forgive you for what you did. I feel that my mother would too."

He hugged her in return, and kissed both of her cheeks. "Go with God's blessing. I'll pray for you every day. You're going to have a fine life. I'm certain of it."

12

"Elise. Have you seen Reese? I stopped by his room a moment ago, to remind him we were supposed to ride a portion of the estate this morning. He's not there. I swear his bed hasn't been slept in."

Elise hurried in from her boudoir, where she'd been dressing to go to the office.

"What do you mean his bed doesn't look slept in? That's impossible. Where would he have slept?"

"I can't imagine. When did you last see him?"

"When I came upstairs to bed. He was at his desk, reading. I told him goodnight and closed his door."

"Well, sometime after that he disappeared. Did he say anything at all? Any hint as to where he might have been going?"

"He was thinking about Chloe. Violette had rung, as you know. So he knew Chloe was in Munich. He's worried about her. When I mentioned she'd been to the police in Germany, it upset him. But I didn't think he was unduly concerned. I tried to reassure him. He knows that Shep is with her. I even told him Chloe would be coming home soon."

"Oh my god, Elise. You don't suppose he's got something into his head about travelling to Germany himself to try to help her? Surely he couldn't be so foolish. He's only fourteen. Why did you decide to tell him anything about Chloe?"

"Sloan, I had to. He was standing right there when Violette rang. He could tell from our conversation that we were talking about his sister. I wasn't going to lie to him. He already feels we shouldn't have lied about the rape and that her biological father was a Nazi."

"Yes, I know. I'm sorry. I didn't mean to sound like I was blaming you for anything. Of course you had to be honest with him. I was going to chat with you about Chloe this morning anyway. I've about decided to pop over to Germany myself. I don't like the idea of her traipsing around a strange country, talking to men who were wretched enough to have assaulted you. We never should have allowed this to get as far as it has. I love Violette, but I'm not certain she acted wisely in this instance."

"Sloan, we're fortunate she's kept us up-to-date. If it weren't for Violette, we'd have no idea where Chloe is. Violette couldn't stop her. Chloe is twenty-two. She would have gone with or without our permission."

"I know. I know. I just feel so helpless. Anything could happen to her. That one chap must be quite a piece of work, from what Violette said. He sounds like he's psychotic. Elise, the more I think about it, I feel I should go to her."

"I'm not against that. But you're forgetting Reese. What about him? Do you think that's what he's done?"

"Where is his passport?"

"In the safe in the library. He knows the combination. You don't suppose . . .?"

"Let's have a look," answered Sloan, as he headed down the staircase

They rushed into the library, and Sloan quickly opened the safe. All of the family passports were kept in a small, metal box, and he immediately grabbed it. Opening it, he flipped through the passports that were lying there. Elise and Sloan. No Reese. And Chloe had her passport with her. Now they knew with certainty. Reese would only have taken his passport if he were planning something extremely foolish – like a trip to Germany without anyone accompanying him.

"Sloan, it isn't here. What are we going to do? We don't even know how long ago he left. He could be in Germany by now."

"I know. Let me think a minute. Does he know where Shep and Chloe are staying in Munich? Does he even know that they're *in* Munich?"

"Yes to both. He continually asks questions. Every time I hear from Violette, he wants to know each and every detail."

"I wonder if he's been planning this for a while. Perhaps he's been gathering information, in preparation for a trip, to act as a hero. God help us. Reese can't do anything to help. He's just a boy."

"Yes, but Sloan, that isn't the way he sees himself. You know that. I doubt if you did at that age either."

"No, I'm sure I didn't. I should call Chloe and Shep in Germany, but we're not supposed to know where they are. Perhaps Chloe wouldn't care about our knowing, since it's about Reese. Anyway, this whole thing is utter foolishness. We *should* know where she is, and we should be able to call anytime."

"Go ahead and call, Sloan. It's the only way we're going to know if Reese is with her. If he isn't, we've got to figure out how we're going to find him. He's somewhere between London and Munich. My sweet boy. Anything could happen to him."

Sloan rang directory assistance, and asked for information about the number for the Bayerischer Hof, in Munich, Germany. After a few moments, the operator gave him a number. Sloan jotted it down and asked her to put him through to the hotel. He could hear the ringing. Then, a man's voice answered, with the name of the establishment. Sloan could speak some German. During the war, he'd attended a special course offered by the RAF, so that pilots could speak and understand the language in the dreaded event that they became captives. He was by no means fluent, but could get by fairly well.

He asked the hotel operator to ring through to Chloe Thornton's room. After three short rings, Chloe picked up the telephone. Sloan was overjoyed to hear his daughter's voice.

"Chloe, it's Daddy," he began.

There was a moment of silence and then Chloe responded. "Daddy? How did you know where to find me?"

"It's a long story. I'll explain everything later. Chloe, your mother and I are very worried about you. I want to come to Munich and bring you home.

Also, we're extremely concerned about Reese. He's disappeared, and so has his passport. That can only mean one thing. He's on his way to Germany to join you, or he's already there. Have you heard from him?"

"Why would Reese do that? How does he even know I'm in Munich? I'm confused. I thought only Viclette knew where we were . . . . Oh. Now I understand. She told you. I should have known better than to trust her. Why can't people just let me live my own life?"

"Chloe. Please stop acting like a child. This is serious. Your parents have a right to be concerned about you. We also have a right to be concerned about Reese. He's only fourteen, for god's sake."

"Well, he isn't here, and I haven't heard from him. Do you want me to ring you if he shows up?"

"I'm going to start a search for him. I won't be here. But, yes, certainly, call Highcroft Hall and leave me a message if you hear anything from him. Mum will be here. I'll start at Heathrow, and continue from there."

"I don't want you to come to Munich. I'm fine. I've learned a lot and am very glad I made the trip. I have things sorted in my head. Shep and I are planning to return very soon. Probably tomorrow. We've just now come back from a meeting with the last of the three men who assaulted Mum. He was by far the best of the three. He's a monk. None of the three has had a happy life. That, in itself, was worth the trip. What they did to Mum has haunted them."

"I'm glad of that, Chloe. Your mother and I will be anxious to hear all about it. But, right now, I'm really worried about Reese. You can understand that. I have to find him. He has no business travelling across the continent alone. So, whether you want me to or not, I need to make a trip to Germany. If I find him before then, I'll ring you. Don't change your plans to return to England. Perhaps, if Reese does make it all the way there, when he finds that you've left he'll turn around and come right home again."

"All right. I'm worried about him, too. He's so young. Shall I check the airport here?"

"I don't think it would do much good, Chloe. They could tell you what planes have come in from London, but that's about all you could learn. I have some contacts here. I can find out more – like whether or not he was a passenger on any flight. I believe he would choose Royal United Kingdom Airways. It's what we've always flown as a family, and thank god I know the president. I'm going to ring him next. I hope there are direct flights to Munich and that he wouldn't have needed to change planes in Paris, Frankfurt, or someplace else."

"Daddy, I'm sorry to have caused all of this upset. I never dreamed Reese would do something like this. Honestly, it never crossed my mind. I still can't understand why he's done it."

"Chloe. He's your bother, and he adores you. It's as simple as that. It doesn't matter to him in the least who fathered you. Just as it doesn't to anyone else. Do you understand?"

Chloe paused. She felt like she'd been stabbed in the heart. Her little brother knew the truth about her paternity, and the only thing he cared about was making certain she was all right. She was the only person who felt differently because of what she'd learned. No one else cared a whit. She was Chloe Thornton. That was all there was to it. Sloan had just further reinforced the conclusion she'd reached after speaking with Brother Pieter. The bond of family was stronger than some stupid genetic link.

"I understand. I do. I've been very foolish and rather self-centred. We need to find Reese, Daddy. Please keep me informed. I pray he shows up here at the hotel, before I depart. I'll leave my door unlocked tonight, so that if he makes it here, he can come right in. They wouldn't give him a key to my room. At least I don't think so."

"Chloe, don't leave your door unlocked. The front desk will call you if he shows up at the hotel. You have to think of your own safety."

"Daddy, this hotel is probably the most beautiful in Munich. I don't worry that anything could happen to me here. But, I'll do as you say. Shep is in the next room. I'll ask him to go down and speak to the front desk so they're alerted. I'll pray that everything turns out all right."

"Right, Chloe. I love you. So does Mum. We'll see this through. Take care of yourself."

Sloan rang off, and Chloe burst into tears. She felt terrible guilt for putting everyone into such a muddle. Although she was glad to have learned so much on the trip, it wouldn't be worth anything at all if her little brother was harmed in any way. She would never forgive herself.

Reese Thornton sat in the Royal United Kingdom Airlines terminal at Orly Airport in Paris. Everything had gone fine thus far, and now all he had to do was connect to his next flight. Then he would be in Munich. He hadn't really been terribly afraid. The ladies who worked on the aeroplanes were very nice and allowed him to have all of the Coca Cola he wanted. He wished he could have just stayed on the aeroplane all the way to Munich, but the one that went straight through had been booked. The only time he'd been a little frightened was when the lady at the counter, where they sold tickets, questioned why he had so much cash with him. Of course, he had to pay for his ticket, which seemed perfectly logical to him, but she thought it was peculiar. There had been an envelope with a lot of money in it inside the safe at home, so he had taken that with him. He had managed to explain everything to the lady's satisfaction, telling her that his parents were meeting him in Germany, and had given him the money for the trip. He told her it was an emergency, and that was why his father hadn't bought his ticket ahead of time. Reese didn't feel guilty, since it wasn't really a lie. It *was* an emergency trip.

He wanted to get to Munich and make Chloe come home with him. Girls had no business travelling on such dangerous missions. Even though Sheppard Sterling was with her, Reese knew Chloe could be very stubborn. Sheppard wouldn't be able to do much if she made up her mind to go in a certain direction. Reese knew that his sister was searching for the men who'd done terrible things to their mother. Who was to say they wouldn't do terrible things to Chloe, too? He wasn't at all certain how he could stop something like that, but Reese was smart and brave, so he'd do whatever it took to keep Chloe safe.

While he sat in the passenger lounge, his father was frantically making telephone calls, in addition to his own travel arrangements. Reese knew that he had undoubtedly caused an uproar. Naturally, he'd known his parents would be frantic, when they found him missing. But he'd thought it would take them longer to put together all of the pieces. He wished he'd left a note, telling them he'd gone someplace else. If they discovered he'd taken his passport, they were certain to figure out that he was on his way to Germany.

Sloan had reached his friend who was with the airline. He'd been most helpful. There were back and forth telephone calls, and finally Sloan learned that his son *had* been aboard a late night flight to Paris, en route to Munich, Germany. Sloan's first thought was to get a message through to the airline to stop Reese from boarding the connecting flight to Munich. In the midst of all the uproar, a frightening thunderstorm began. Each time he made a call, the line was filled with static. It was irritating, to say the least. Elise was weeping, while pacing up and down, worried sick, and Sloan's nerves were frayed.

Just as he'd connected with the airline to ask that they detain his son, the line went dead. There had been an enormous clap of thunder and a huge flash of lightening. A moment later the electricity was lost, and all of the lights went out. It wasn't an infrequent occurrence in Thornton-on-Sea. London was probably perfectly all right, but small villages were more prone to such interruptions. Sloan slammed his hand down and shouted, "Bloody hell!" Elise was startled by his outburst, but when the lights went out she realised the cause. She sank down on a settee by the telephone, sobbing. Sloan put his arms around her, holding her close.

"It will be all right, Elise. Reese isn't a fool. He'll be fine. The power shouldn't be off terribly long. Do you want me to drive to London, and speak to the airline people there?"

"No. Absolutely not. The weather is wretched, and I'm not going to add you to my list of people to worry about. We're going to have to calm down, and wait it out. What a maddening dilemma."

"It is. But, we have to remember that we've raised two intelligent, sensible children – for the most part. They're not fools. Let's try to look on the bright side. We're probably in a frantic mindset for no good reason. As soon as I can, I'll get back with the airlines. They said that his connecting flight to Munich would be taking off in one hour. If we're fortunate, we'll get the power back long before that."

13

Chloe scurried to Shep's room. She rapped sharply on the door, and it only took a moment for him to open it. It was clear he'd been having a lie-down. His hair was mussed and his eyes looked sleepy.

"Chloe. What's going on? You never come over here at night."

"I know, Shep. But something has happened. My brother is missing. He's taken his passport and disappeared. My father thinks he's on his way here. Reese thinks he's going to save me from some awful mishap."

"Did your father ring you? How did he know where to find you? I'm confused."

"Well, it's apparent that Violette told him. I suppose she's been in touch all along. We shouldn't really be surprised. Anyway, it doesn't matter. I explained to Daddy that I've got my head sorted out. He knows we're planning a return trip. The important thing now is my brother."

"I'm surprised Reese would do something so stupid. He's old enough to know better."

"Oh, Shep. He's old enough to think he can intervene if I'm in some sort of danger. You know how boys that age are."

"Right. I do. Sorry for the remark about his being stupid. I'd have done the same thing if it were my sister. Egad. I'm here, aren't I? And I'm a lot older than Reese. So then, what are we to do?"

"I don't know. I want you to go down to the desk and talk to the night clerk. Tell him that if a young boy shows up asking about me, they should ring my room at once. I was going to leave my room unlocked so he could get in, if he didn't stop at the desk. He might just call and get the room number. But my father said no to that idea."

"He's right. Even if Reese did come straight to your room, he'd knock on the door. There's no reason to leave the door unlocked."

"I wanted to make absolutely certain he could get in right away."

"Don't do it, Chloe. It's foolish and there's no need."

"All right, Shep. Will you please hurry, and go down to the desk?"

"Yes, of course."

Shep was still dressed, although it was quite late. Both had decided to turn in early, since they had a long trip the next day. Apparently he'd fallen asleep before undressing. He smoothed his hair back and gave Chloe a peck on the cheek.

"Don't worry, Pip. Everything will be fine. Are you hungry? While I'm downstairs, I could run and pick up something to eat. It would save having to wait for room service."

"Yes. Good. I *am* hungry. I don't want to leave the room, that's for certain. In case Reese shows up."

"I know. I'll only be a tick. Don't worry."

Shep left, and Chloe returned to her own room. She sat down on the edge of the bed and fidgeted. How in the world had all of this come about? Only a few weeks before she'd been getting ready to sit for her exams, looking forward to a peaceful summer in Thornton-on-Sea with her family. One, overheard conversation had turned her world upside down. It was amazing to think about everything that had happened since that moment. Finding each of the former Nazis had been nothing short of miraculous. They had all been so different than she'd imagined. Except for Wolfgang. *He* was exactly what she'd imagined. However, apparently that wasn't the real Wolfgang. He was still a brute, in her opinion. She felt the sorriest for Dieter. No matter what he'd done, she would never have wished such terrible injuries on anyone. She also felt sorry for Pieter. He wasn't an evil man. Perhaps only a weak one. At least, back when it had all happened. The strength he'd shown since, in giving up a normal life as penance for his sins, was anything but weak. It was strange to have to confess that someone who had violated her mother had also taught her a valuable lesson in life. Chloe had to admit that not one of them was the same person he'd been at the time of the assault. Pieter, particularly, had touched her heart. He would have made a fine teacher. It was a shame that one mistake in life, albeit one that could have earned him a hanging, had robbed the world of a person who might have had a great influence on young people.

Chloe heard a noise in the hallway and then a rattling of her door. She leaped up and unlocked the bolt. It was undoubtedly Shep, returning with his arms too full to knock. As soon as the lock was released, the door opened. A hand came through, reached around the doorframe, and flicked off the overhead light. Chloe jumped back onto the bed. What was going on? Surely Shep wouldn't try to frighten her, when things were so difficult already. She called out his name, but there was no answer. She felt panicky. She opened her mouth to scream, and a hand fastened over it. Chloe squirmed and struggled to get away.

"Be calm, my pretty daughter. I don't intend to cause you any harm. Fathers should teach their daughters about the joys of intimacy. That's one of our most important duties. I want you to lie still, while I show you how it's done. You'll find that it's the most spectacular experience of your life."

Chloe was terrified. My god. He meant to rape her, just as he had her mother. He truly *was* mad. How could she have been lulled into a false belief about him? Where was Shep? What could she do? She couldn't scream. The intruder had taken a piece of cloth and stuffed it into her mouth. She continued to kick her legs and thrash about. None of her movements made any difference to him.

"Don't fight me. I promise you'll enjoy what I'm about to teach you. How else can a daughter learn? You haven't let any other man touch you, have you? I don't think so. You're so obviously an innocent. That's one reason I'm so proud that you're my daughter."

Chloe managed to free one hand from his grip. She slapped him hard across the face. Then she yanked the gag from her mouth.

"Get away from me you filthy pig. I'm not your daughter."

She began to scream, but he hit her on the side of the head. She blacked out. When she came round, he had bound her hands and feet. All she could do was pray that Shep would arrive in time. The ogre crawled on top of her. She continued to writhe and squirm. He managed to pull up her nightdress, and she was exposed.

Oh God. Oh God. This fiend is going to do the same thing to me that he did to Mum. Oh, please God, please save me, she prayed to herself.

Tears were streaming from her eyes. Was this the way her mother had felt? She could feel his sour breath on her face. Just as he reached down to perform the disgusting act, the light suddenly came on. Her attacker blinked in the abrupt illumination. A bedside lamp came smashing down on his head. His body went limp and fell to the side. Chloe looked up to see her brother Reese. He quickly untied her and she fell into his outstretched arms.

"Reese. Reese. I can't believe this. How did you know where I was? Why didn't the desk ring me? Oh my god, Reese, this disgusting creature is one of the men who raped our mother."

Reese looked at the crumpled heap, lying across the bed. Pieter's priestly robes were in disarray, and his underwear was lowered. He'd yielded to the temptation that he'd spoken about at the monastery. Chloe was repulsed. She had actually felt trust and pity for the man.

"Everything will be all right now, Chloe. It's a good thing I came. Where is Sheppard? I thought he was supposed to be keeping you safe?"

"Reese, he's out getting us food. Please, quit talking so calmly, and call the police."

"I shall. I'll ring the desk and have them send hotel security. But don't worry. If he comes round, I'll bash him again with the lamp. I hit him awfully hard. I think he'll be out for a good while."

Chloe was trembling from head to toe, but she couldn't help smiling. Her little brother had saved the day. Not her *half*-brother, or her *half-sibling*. Her *brother*.

Hotel Security came and took Brother Pieter away. He was conscious by that time, but they said they were going to send him to hospital to make certain there was no serious head injury. They praised Reese's quick thinking and credited him with saving his sister from sexual assault. Later it came to light that there were several missing girls around the area in which Pieter lived, and the authorities were looking into each one of the cases. Who knew what might have happened to Chloe?

As soon as the security men left, with Pieter in tow, Chloe rang her father. She wasn't able to make the connection, and learned that the power was out in Thornton-on-Sea. Asking that the operator keep trying, Chloe lay down on the bed, still shaking. Finally, Shep returned, arms loaded with food. Everyone was far too excited and wound up to eat. Chloe ran to him, throwing her arms around his neck.

"Oh, Shep. Thank God you're back. You won't believe everything that's happened."

Shep was confused when he saw Reese. Pieter had already left with the security men, so he had no way of knowing the drama that had unfolded.

"Slow down, Chloe. Take a deep breath, and tell me everything slowly, so I can understand," he implored.

Chloe sat down in a chair and waited a few moments, until she was able to relax a bit. Then she gave him the entire account of everything that had happened.

"I wouldn't be quite so surprised if it had been Wolfgang. He's obviously a complete psycho. But I *am* surprised it was Pieter. He must be even more bonkers than Wolfgang. I almost liked that chap."

"Shep, how is it possible that I felt as if he'd solved a lot of my confusion? He's the one who made an awful lot of sense. This makes me question my judgment."

"No, Chloe. Just because the chap has definite problems, when it comes to self-control and god knows what else, it doesn't mean he hasn't some perfectly rational times. He *did* make sense. He was spot on about Sloan being your only father. All of the foolishness he was spouting, about having to teach his daughter lessons in intimacy, was his way of convincing himself that what he intended to do wasn't evil. Don't throw out the baby with the bathwater, Chloe. Accept the points he made about your mother's happiness in life, versus his and the others. That was completely true. What he tried to do tonight only proves it all the more. It's all over now. Your little brother is the hero."

Reese beamed. "I knew if I could get to Germany, I'd be able to protect you. Course, I didn't know some perv was going to break into your room and the like. I'm just glad I got here when I did."

"Your timing was perfect, Sherlock," Chloe laughed and cuddled him. She was still terribly shaken, but didn't want to let Reese see her upset.

"Weren't you frightened travelling all the way from England alone?" Shep asked.

"Well, yes. I'm glad I won't have to go back by myself. I was mostly afraid that Dad would find me. I kept watching the faces of the people who worked at the airline desk. Every time they got a phone call, I was afraid I was going to be sent back home."

"You would have been, Reese. The last time I talked to Dad, he told me he was going to search for you. He knows the head of the airline, so it was only a matter of time. I think the only reason you got here was because the phone and electricity are out in Thornton-on-Sea. Poor Mum and Dad. They must be mad with worry."

Chloe turned to Shep. "Are we going to have to stay longer now, because of what Pieter did? I suppose the police will want to interview us."

"Yes, I suspect. But if we can do that early in the morning, we should be able to fly home later in the day. Certainly by nightfall."

"I'll be so happy to see England. This has been a nightmare."

"I've rather enjoyed myself," Shep smiled. "How else would I have had you all to myself for such a long time?"

Chloe gave Shep a warning glance. She didn't want Reese to get ideas. Shep turned to Reese and smiled. "Just joking, old chap. But I have to admit I grew rather fond of your sister during this little adventure."

"I can tell she feels the same way, because she's blushing. She doesn't do that very often."

Shep laughed. "Well, something very good may have come out of this nightmare."

Chloe smiled. She couldn't deny it. She would miss having Shep close by when they returned to England.

"Shep. Perhaps we can spend time at each other's houses during the rest of the summer. I have to go to Hertfordshire in early September. Do you think you could visit me there?"

Shep grinned. "Just say the word, Pip, and I'll be there."

"What's this 'Pip' stuff?" asked Reese.

"It's my nickname for your sister. I had a dog named Pip. She told me Shep sounds like a dog's name, so I gave her a canine label of her own. Just a bit of fun, Reese."

"I like it. I think I'll start calling you Pip, too."

"No. You can't do that, little chum. That name is reserved for my use only. You'll have to find your own tag for her."

"I've always called her Sissy. I think I'll stick with that."

Chloe hugged him tightly. "That's the best name a brother can give a sister. I love it, and don't you ever stop calling me that."

AFTERWORD

Chloe Thornton was dressed and ready to begin her walk toward the altar of the chapel at Highcroft Hall. Her handsome father, Sloan, stood waiting to take her arm. Shortly before, she had kissed her mother, as she proceeded Chloe down the aisle. She could see Shep standing at the far end, awaiting her arrival. She loved him so, and was terribly anxious to become his wife.

During the past year, while she had been doing her internship, Shep had spent a lot of time in Hertfordshire with her. Their love had grown, and the day finally arrived when he'd slipped a ring on her finger and asked her to share the rest of her life with him. She had graduated, and then planned the wedding. Afterwards, they would be making their home in Sterling-Mendip, where Chloe was planning on opening her own, private veterinary practice.

While still in her bedroom at Highcroft Hall, dressing for the wedding, a package had arrived addressed to Chloe and her mother Chloe had almost left it unopened, assuming it was simply another wedding gift and that it could wait until after the service. Then, she looked at the return address and saw that it was from Germany. She tore open the paper, and was astounded to see a book emerge from the wrappings. The book was entitled *The Folly of War*, and the author was Dieter Schwab. There was a photo of him on the cover.

The inside flap of the book said that after a visit from a young English girl the previous summer, he had been moved to write the tale of his life before and after the awful experience he'd had while serving as a Nazi soldier. It spoke of lessons he'd learned and of the things that really mattered in life. Dieter had written on the flyleaf of the book – "To Chloe Thornton, My inspiration and salvation. I shall never forget you, and the impact you had on my life. With Warm Regards, Dieter Schwab."

Chloe handed the book to her mother, whose eyes filled with tears. She had written the man a letter of forgiveness after Chloe's return from Germany. Both she and Chloe hugged one another. Looking into each other's eyes, Chloe said "Mum. I'm so glad I made the trip. More importantly, I'm glad you wrote the letter. Dieter took my advice. I told him that he could be an inspiration to others about the folly of war. He used my words. I pray that this book will change his life, and that he will find that he does have a purpose."

"I'm glad you made the trip, too. It was frightening, but much good came from it. I never thought I'd say those words. How appropriate that you received the book today of all days."

Chloe smiled. She placed the book tenderly in her travelling case, so that she could read it on her wedding trip. Then she turned again to her mother.

"I know who I am, Mum, and I want to thank you for the sacrifices you made for me all of your life I hope I can be as fine a mother someday as you have been. I hope Shep will be the wonderful daddy that I've had. I know he will be, although he has very big shoes to fill. I'm so sorry that I ever hurt either one of you. But, I think we've all learned an important lesson. If I'm fortunate enough to have children, I intend to tell them the entire story of my birth. There will be no more secrets in this family. Now," she sighed happily, "my daddy is waiting at the door to the chapel. I need to go and tell him that he was my very first love."

OTHER BOOKS BY MARY CHRISTIAN PAYNE

The Somerville Trilogy

Willow Grove Abbey: Book 1 of the Somerville Trilogy
St. James Road: Book 2 of the Somerville Trilogy
Serendipity: Book 3 of the Somerville Trilogy

The Claybourne Trilogy

The White Feather: Book 1 of the Claybourne Trilogy
The White Butterfly: Book 2 of the Claybourne Trilogy
White Cliffs of Dover: Book 3 of the Claybourne Trilogy

The Thornton Trilogy

No Regrets: Book 1 of The Thornton Trilogy
No Gentleman: Book 2 of the Thornton Trilogy
No Secrets: Book 3 of the Thornton Trilogy

ABOUT THE AUTHOR

M ary Christian Payne was highly successful in several management positions in Fortune 500 Companies, in New York City, St. Louis, Missouri, Orlando Florida, and Tulsa, Oklahoma. Her work included Grant writing, and designing and writing Training Manuals for Executive Training Programs.

She left the corporate world, and became Director of Career Development at the Women' Resource Center at the University of Tulsa, where she designed a program that enabled hundreds of adult women to return to college and better their lives. She received the Mayor's Pinnacle Award in 1993 for this achievement. Mary left that position when the Center closed, and then opened her own Career Counseling Center. She retired in 2008.

Mary Christian Payne became a successful, best-selling author at the age of 71, with the help of her publisher, Tom Corson-Knowles. All of her life, she had wanted to write, and had received accolades for her unpublished work. She was encouraged in college, and writing was a significant part of the various jobs she held.

In 2013, she read Tom Corson-Knowles' book about publishing on Kindle. She wrote to him and he telephoned her. The rest is history. Since that time, she has published nine books, with more on the way.

Mary lost her husband in June, 2015, after 33 years of marriage. The grief process brought a lull to her writing, but she found that putting words on paper helped immensely. She is now in the process of writing her second novel since his death. She lives in Tulsa, Oklahoma, with her two beloved Maltese dogs.

Sign up for the newsletter to get news, updates and new release info from Mary Christian Payne:

http://bit.ly/MaryChristianPayne

ONE LAST THING...

If you enjoyed this book, I'd be very grateful if you'd post a short review on Amazon. Your support really does make a difference and I read all the reviews personally.

Thanks again for your support!